NINA HAYES

The Holly Homicide

The Old Bat Chronicles Book 2

*To Lora O'Brien, who gave me Greta Goode
Thanks for all you do to keep the magic alive.*

Contents

Preface

Welcome back to Bramble Lane!

As ever, the story of Eve and her friends is interwoven with authentic Irish folk magic, and folklore. This time with a Christmas theme, and lots of local colour. So for those of you interested in the background, there's a section at the end of the book, explaining the practices and beliefs mentioned in the tale.

Before you dive in, however, it might be of use to read

the glossary below. As an Irish author, writing about Irish people, I use some slang and some Hiberno-English phrases and words that might be unfamiliar, but they are part of the natural rhythm of speech here. And I know you like to add to your vocabulary of colourful Irish sayings! Also please see any typos or mistakes as proof that this story came from the heart of a human, and not the imperfect perfection of AI.

I also use UK English spellings, in general.

I've provided a short cast list, so you can keep the main characters in mind. If you prefer to be surprised by new characters, skip that bit!

This story is set in December, in the run up to Christmas. This is a very special season in Ireland, with lots of folklore surrounding it. On Christmas Eve, many people still place candles in their porch or windows, to signify a welcome and in remembrance of those who can't be with us. In the weeks leading up to the holidays, people return home from all over the world, and while Eve's children are only travelling relatively short distance, I've tried to capture some of the anticipation and bittersweet moments experienced by the parents of adult children.

I hope you'll enjoy the story and whatever time of year it is you find yourself reading The Holly Homicide, may some of the magic of the season find its way into your life.

Glossary:

Amadán A foolish person (see **Eejit**)

Bean Feasa Wise Woman - The Irish equivalent of a "witch" - but with very clear roles in society. See back of book for further info.

Brí The natural wild energy of a place

Bua The energy a place develops through human use

Eejit: A complete twit, a foolish person

Gossoon A young lad

Garda (s) Gardaí (p) : An Irish policeman is a Garda and the plural is Gardaí. The force itself is An Garda Siochána, Guardians of the Peace.

Púca: A mischievous otherworldly spirit.

And if there are any words you don't understand, feel free to email author@celebratingwords.com. I love to hear from readers.

<u>CAST</u>

Eve Caulton, 50-ish, Artist and owner of Kimberly Cottage

The Old Bat(s)

Dymphna Moriarty, Next Door Neighbour and the unofficial leader of the Wise Women

Niamh Caulton neé Boyd, Eve's mother

Claudia Warren, Brigadier General of the Irish Women's Brigade

Greta Goode, incorrigible, famous for her true crime podcast Greta's Gory Truths

Neighbours

Tom MacDonagh (Retired)

Detective Ronan Desmond (Garda)

Margaret Fury (Teacher)

The Marrinans, Ellen and Finn, with their kids Boyd (16) and Melly (14)

Ashleigh and Sean (Pine Tree Road)

Others

Professor Eithne Blennerville (Leinster University)
Dr. Murray (Leinster University)
and the rest...well, you'll have to meet them as they come!

vi

Acknowledgement

Grateful thanks as ever to the wonderful beta readers without whom I would be lost.

Especial thanks to Joe Lysaght, whose eagle eyes and recommendations are always welcome.

Chapter 1

Eve Caulton hung a gold and red bauble on the tree and stepped back to cast a critical eye over her handiwork. The tree filled the corner of her living room, standing to one side of the fireplace. It was the first time in her adult life that she had chosen a real tree, and her first Christmas in Kimberly Cottage. Somehow an artificial one didn't seem right for the old place. When her friend and neighbour Tom had recommended a living tree - a tree planted in a container rather than cut down - she had been intrigued.

"You can plant it out or return it to be planted on forestry land," Tom had explained. "They're quite neat, perfect for the living rooms in our cottages. And you can keep it in its container, use it for years."

His enthusiasm sold her on the idea and now, smelling the fresh pine aroma in her house, she was doubly glad that she had opted for the real thing. As a bonus, they had had a lovely trip to Cork to pick out two trees, one for Kimberly Cottage and one for Tom's cottage close by on Bramble Lane. Rowan Tree House was a cottage identical to Kimberly, both being one of six built in Victorian times, before the leafy Merrion suburb had become part of Dublin city. Back then it was a rural village, popular with those who wanted to live outside the city and home to working farms, all long since eaten up by housing estates and business development.

In her old life, there would have been no question of a real tree. Her ex-husband Peter hated them and had insisted on ultra modern, synthetic trees in whatever colour was currently fashionable. As a result, she had endured silver, blue, purple and even black trees, expertly decorated in complementary colours by a series of superior young women from his office. All very elegant but not what you would call "warm" or "homely," and Eve thought her neat little Nordman Fir was a vast improvement.

For her new tree she had dug out an eclectic mix of decorations, long hidden in the attic in her old house and rescued by Eve before she had to sell it. They included baubles her mother Niamh had given her, some of which her late father had given Niamh for their first Christmas as husband and wife. There was a painted clay ball that Eve herself had made as a child, an early indicator of her artistic talent preserved by her proud parents. While clearing the attic, Eve had also retrieved a set of funny, clay ornaments that her children Mairead and Liam had given her one year. She smiled at the memory of the pair working away in secret and shyly presenting their inexpertly wrapped gift. She had insisted on placing them on the tree that year, despite Peter's objections but he had hidden them after Christmas. Now she could hang them in pride of place, and no one could object. This was her home, and she could do as she pleased.

She had bought some new baubles as well: Newbridge silver ornaments, handmade Waterford Glass balls and a cheerful ceramic Santa with a cheeky smile. And finally she committed what Peter would have termed an unforgivable sin against good taste - she threw lengths of tinsel around the sturdy branches, watching them glint and wink in the firelight. It was already almost dark, the winter evenings drawing in quickly as they entered December. But despite the dim light and cold weather, the living room was cheerful, colourful and warm. To Eve's artistic eye, the tree was a work of art in its own, cheerful way.

With a happy sigh, Eve took a few photographs of the tree and sent them to her daughter Mairead.

"Decorating finally finished, see you soon!" she texted. In exactly one month it would be Christmas Eve, and both her children would be arriving for a week's visit. Liam was easy going and happy to sleep on the sofa but Mairead liked her comfort so the spare room had been primped, plumped and prepped to the highest level. Mairead, she knew, worried about her the most, fearing she would be lonely or nervous living alone. Admittedly she had got off to a rocky start when she first moved in, but the least said about that the better. Now she just wanted Mairead to feel comfortable and enjoy her visit. If a hand embroidered quilt and matching pillowcases did the trick, it was well worth it.

"Liam can sleep in mine," Tom had offered, but at least for the first few nights Eve wanted him under the same roof. If he got sick of the sofa in a few days, she could always ask Tom to put him up for the rest of the week. She couldn't stop smiling as she thought about the three of them, sitting around the fire, catching up on each other's lives. Mince pies, a huge box of chocolates, and homemade Christmas cake - everything would be perfect.

No sooner had she allowed herself that thought, than she heard a loud noise in her back garden. To be accurate, it sounded as if half her back fence had collapsed and then someone or something had kicked over her planters. Eve wrenched open the back door to find that in fact half the back portion of her fence *was* now hanging askew, with quite a few planks broken and splintered. It separated her garden from the overgrown wasteland at the back of Bramble Lane. She looked around her garden in dismay, letting out a yelp when she saw two large planters were indeed overturned, toppled by the falling boards.

"Eve!" Her next door neighbour, Dymphna Moriarty called out from her own garden. "Are you alright?"

"I'm fine," Eve replied, "But my garden looks like a bomb went off!"

Dymphna's head appeared over the wooden fence that divided their property at the back. "So I see! What on earth happened?"

"I don't know! I was minding my own business, decorating my tree, when this happened! I heard a commotion and ran out, but - well, look at it."

Dymphna shook her head and sighed. "It's a mess. I'll give Tom a shout, see if he can come over. You'll need to fix that fence as soon as possible, I wouldn't like to have an opening like that between me and the wilderness."

Wilderness was an exaggeration, Bramble Lane being part of one of Dublin's most exclusive suburbs, however it *was* disconcerting to have a gaping hole in her fence, and nothing beyond it but several acres of tangled brambles and thorns. It was rare nowadays, but the space between Bramble Lane and the main Merrion Road was a large undeveloped area, bordered by thorns, undergrowth, and trees.

Eve retreated to her kitchen locking the back door securely

behind her. Within a few minutes, to her relief, both Dymphna and Tom were on the doorstep. Tom was - well, her friend and neighbour. But also, more than that. Possibly.

"I'll go out and take a look around," Tom declared. He'd arrived clutching his tool kit and several sturdy looking lengths of wood. Eve smiled. This was one of the reasons she liked him so much. He never wasted time in hand-wringing, but just stepped up and did whatever he could to help. She could relax knowing there would be some kind of repair to the fence before it was too dark to work.

Dymphna made a beeline for Eve's kitchen, as at home in Kimberly Cottage as she was in her own, Vespertilio Cottage. Like Eve's mother, she was what, in bygone days, would have been called a Wise Woman, or in Irish, a Bean Feasa, with some very special skills. She was used to being a necessary, if not always welcome, visitor in times of need. In the neighbourhood, she was the undisputed - if unelected - leader of the *other ladies with special skills*, and the person most ordinary persons turned to for advice and help.

In Eve's house however, she was like a member of the family. Her long friendship with Niamh, Eve's mother, ensured that she would have kept an eye out for Eve anyway, but as it turned out, she had quickly become very fond of the gentle artist. Eve's first days on Bramble Lane had been eventful, the quiet suburb rocked by an unprecedented murder, but the culprit was under lock and key and all was now well.

She frowned as she made a pot of tea and raided Eve's cupboards for something nice to put with it.

"Have you no biscuits in the house?"

"Under the sink," Eve called back, "I hide them there so I won't munch on them all the time."

Dymphna rolled her eyes. "Daft."

She retrieved a packet of chocolate biscuits from a box marked "Cleaning Products," and arranged them on a plate, then on a small tray flanked by steaming mugs of strong tea. "Here we go, this will calm the nerves. How's Tom getting on out there?"

Eve accepted a cup of tea gratefully. "He's doing alright, as far as I can see. It's almost dark but he says he'll be finished before it's too dim to see. I'll have to get someone in to fix it properly tomorrow though, I can't have half the back fence blowing over every time there's a high wind!"

"I can't imagine what caused it, unless a Púca was passing through."

Eve knew Dymphna could be joking but equally, she might be dead serious. Púca were mischievous creatures, famous in Irish folklore and Eve was old enough to remember her grandparents' deep belief in such things. Belief that was rooted in personal experience and living traditions. But here in the modern city of Dublin, in these times of internet and mobile phones, it seemed highly unlikely that passing fairies had chosen her garden to mess up. The answer was far more likely to be mundane.

Tom MacDonagh ambled in the back door, looking very pleased with himself.

"A good job, if I say so myself. That fence isn't going anywhere tonight. I'll ring the Merrion Garden Centre in the morning, there's a young fella there who does jobs like fencing."

"Thanks so much, Tom. Any idea what caused it?"

Tom frowned. "To be honest, it looks like someone took a hammer to it. Or maybe a mallet. There are marks all over the planks, it looks like they took a battering before they came down. It's too dark to see properly, but I'll try and see more in the morning."

Eve thanked him, feeling a wave of gratitude that he was there for her to rely on. It wasn't just because they were particularly close, inching their way towards a romance that was all the sweeter for being unexpected. No, a large part of Tom's charm for her was that he would do as much, and be as helpful, to a complete stranger.

And while she was a mature woman, with a lifetime's experience behind her, completely independent and not at all in *need* of a man - she wasn't stupid and knew a good thing when it appeared bearing homegrown vegetables and wielding a hammer. Putting aside thoughts of the damage to her garden, she pointed out her newly decorated tree and talk turned to the coming festivities.

It was a small step from that to exchanging tit-bits of news about friends and neighbours. Their friend Claudia had successfully quashed a rebellion among the younger members of the Irish Women's Brigade, who wanted to produce a new style of calendar for the organization, featuring good-looking young people in arty settings. "No," Claudia had said firmly. "People expect nice pictures of home baking and crafts. If they wanted edgy fashionistas, they would hardly be looking on the Brigade website, now would they?"

Another of Niamh and Dymphna's cronies had been featured on the national radio station, promoting her true crime podcast, Greta's Gory Truths. Greta Goode was an incorrigible auld woman, said Dymphna, but you had to admit, she had listeners eating out of her hand. Ever since her appeal on air had helped solve the crime that had rocked the peace of their little street, her ratings had doubled. Now Greta was enjoying herself mightily.

"Well, I have a piece of news," Tom said smugly, "I bet neither of you know -"

"Is it about the new neighbours?" Dymphna said calmly.

Tom stared at her.

"Well, that knocked the wind out of my sails. Yes, and I thought I was the first to know."

"Her daughter Una," Eve took pity on him. "She works in the estate agents, remember? She sold me this place, and I bet, she sold the O'Reilly's house too."

The O'Reilly house, one of the cottages on Bramble Lane, had become vacant due to unfortunate circumstances, earlier that year.

Tom grinned. "Ah, I should have guessed. Well, it's your news then, Mrs. Moriarty. You have the inside story."

He was rewarded with one of Dymphna's rare smiles. "Una did let me know that the house has sold," she conceded. "And it's rather exciting. The family are Irish-American."

"Really?" Eve wasn't sure what she had expected, but nothing so exotic.

"His grandfather was Irish, from somewhere in Connaught. He's a property developer, owns some land here in Dublin according to Una. She's Irish, from Kilkenny. She moved to New York almost twenty years ago, met your man and settled down in Chicago. They have two kids, in their teens, sixteen and fourteen. The boy's the eldest and the girl is the younger one. They moved back to have a nicer quality of life for their kids."

"Wait, they moved to a two bed-roomed cottage, all four of them? Won't that be a bit cramped?"

"Una did point that out," Dymphna shrugged. "They're going

to extend the house, she said. But they said their priority was to be in this area, to be close to her mother. Poor old thing is getting on in years. She's nearly seventy."

Eve and Tom looked at the eighty-two year old Dymphna and tried not to make eye contact with each other. The usual rules of aging didn't seem to apply to her, or to Eve's mother, or any of their cronies.

The six houses of Bramble Lane, built to provide artisan workers with accommodation in the late Victorian period, weren't large but had extensive gardens. Eve supposed the newcomers were willing to sacrifice a little bit of lawn and flowerbeds for an extra bedroom.

"So, they'll put up with a small house. That's nice, they sound like they'll fit right in."

The denizens of Bramble Lane were a close knit bunch, especially after recent events. Any family willing to put up with a little inconvenience to look after an elderly mother would receive a warm welcome and lots of helping hands. Especially as they were returning from abroad - the Irish habit of hospitality and welcome, the *"céad míle fáilte,"* or hundred thousand welcomes, was deeply ingrained.

"What's their name?" Eve asked. "We can stop calling the house "the O'Reilly's," now."

"Marrinan," Dymphna said. "And Una says they plan to revert to the original name. The house used to be called Holly Cottage."

Eve smiled. "New neighbours for Christmas, in Holly Cottage. Perfect."

Chapter 2

Next morning, another neighbour called to Eve's door. Ronan Desmond lived a few doors down in Copper Beech Cottage, an earnest young man with a reserved manner. This aloofness came from his job, which had once been a closely guarded secret from the residents of Bramble Lane.

Ronan was in fact a Detective Garda Sergeant.

This interesting fact had emerged during the rather unfortunate events earlier in the year. The detective had learned to be grateful for the help Dymphna and friends could provide. Thanks to their intervention, Ronan was now happily courting the young local schoolteacher, Margaret Fury. As Margaret occupied yet another of the six cottages the romance was of great interest locally . Speculation was high as to whether Ronan would ask Margaret to move in to his cottage, or would they perhaps move to hers, and if so, what would become of the empty house? And would there be talk, perhaps, of a wedding?Or perhaps it was too soon for them to contemplate any major move?

Opinion was divided, pretty evenly.

"Nonsense," said Mrs. Moriarty to any such talk. "I knew within two dates that I would marry my Frank. You can be too cautious. Sure, people date for years and still break up."

"They do," opined Claudia, "But have you never heard the saying, "*Marry in haste, repent at leisure?*""

"Hmm. If you buy a pig in a poke, you'll repent - whether you took all day to decide or not."

Privately, Eve was inclined to agree with Dymphna.

She had spent years with her ex-husband Peter before they became engaged, then waited another two years to marry and look at her now! Peter was on wife number two, the glamourous if gullible Liza, and she was…well, happier than she had been in a long time, to be honest. She didn't regret her marriage but she thought two people as well suited as Ronan and Margaret might as well enjoy life, while they were still young.

Not that Ronan looked much like a man enjoying life, she thought to herself. He looked harassed and faintly perplexed.

"Morning, Ronan."

"Morning, Eve. I hear you had some trouble last night."

"You heard about that?"

Of course, everyone heard about anything that happened on Bramble Lane.

"Yeah, my back fence came down."

"Mind if I come in? You're not the only one who had a spot of bother last night, and I'm taking statements."

"Of course, come in. But I don't know how much use it'll be."

Eve settled Ronan in an armchair and once he had admired her tree, and was presented with a mug of coffee, she regaled him with the story of her desecrated garden. "Two large planters, Ronan, completely overturned. And the fence is in bits."

"Tom did a good job on it," Ronan smiled at her look of

surprise. "I was out in the field at the back, earlier today. There's a couple of fences destroyed on the far side too, the back of houses on the main road. Very similar to yours, half the planks down and a bit of damage to gardens. Someone, or something, went on the rampage last night."

Eve thought of Dymphna and her comment about the Púca. "Something, you say?"

"Well there are hoof marks on several of the planks, or at least, that's the best description I can give of it. Possibly a steel toed boot, at a pinch. Maybe some kind of odd shaped mallet. But "hoof print"is the closest. I wondered if kids were keeping horses around here, but there's no sign of it."

In some parts of Dublin, youngsters still kept horses as pets or for racing. Eve had once seen a horse pulling a racing carriage down the motorway, pursued by two Garda cars. It wasn't unheard of, but she had never seen any sign of horses around Merrion.

"It doesn't seem likely," she agreed. "And if it was a horse, where is it now? Could it have escaped through one of the other gardens?"

Ronan shook his head. "No, there's no way through from the back to the front. More than likely it's just a bunch of teenagers, up to mischief. But if you hear anything outside, call me or call the local station. I've let them know what's happening. They'll send someone round to check it."

Eve thanked him, and he took his leave. She had a busy day ahead, between painting and teaching. She had received two valuable commissions for paintings to be given as Christmas presents, both of which were nearly finished but required some last touches. In the afternoon, she would be teaching art in the local community centre. In addition to her work at the Adult Learning Centre, she had been offered a class at the smaller, run-on-a-shoestring budget parish hall. The pay was minuscule, but the real reward was the satisfaction of seeing both young and old would-be painters blossom. The class was a mixture of retirees and teenagers, who would probably never mix in the usual course of things. In her class, they chatted freely and exchanged lively and sometimes hilarious opinions on a wide range of topics. Some of them were even shaping up to be decent artists.

She lost herself in her work until a knock at the front door broke her concentration.

"Eve?" Tom peered through the living room window, and she hastened to open the front door. His hands were full with two bags and a quantity of small planks, explaining why he hadn't just rung the doorbell. Beside him stood a young man, dressed in work gear, similarly laden. "Howya, love. This is Luke. From the Merrion Garden Centre."

"Ah, the young man who does fences?" Eve stepped aside, and waved them inside. "Please come in."

Luke looked around the little house, his interest obvious.

"I've always wondered what they looked like on the inside," he remarked. "I love these old cottages. Well, any old houses, to be honest. I'd love one like this."

"You might have to wait a while," Eve smiled. "They don't come up for sale often. I was very lucky to get Kimberly Cottage, and the only other one that has been available in recent years was sold recently."

"Oh! Yes, our new neighbours. I can't wait." Tom rubbed his hands together. "They sound ideal, don't you think? And kids, won't it be lovely to have young people on Bramble Lane?"

"I saw they took the For Sale sign down," Luke said. "I

delivered some fencing to Copper Beech Cottage yesterday , and I noticed it was gone. Ah well, there goes my dream of winning the lottery and moving in!"

He grinned, and jerked his head towards the back of the house.

"Shall we? Tom said his repair job wouldn't stand up to much, and there's bad weather forecast for tomorrow."
Eve nodded gratefully, and led the way to the back garden. Luke's eyes widened as he took in the amount of damage done to the fence, but he made no further remarks. Instead he set to work, Tom acting as his helper, and Eve retreated to the kitchen to put on the kettle. As she fished the good biscuits out of their hiding place, it occurred to her to wonder how much the new fence was going to cost.

"I'm an eejit," she chided herself, "I should have asked. But then again, I can't have it falling down the next time we have high winds!"

She put out three cups, and a plate of goodies, then paused for a moment. On impulse she added another cup - just as there was a familiar knock on the door.

"Eve?" Her mother Niamh could never be persuaded to ring before calling in to visit, and in self defense Eve had developed a sixth sense about her impromptu appearances. She couldn't resist a smug look as she opened the door to Niamh, with the greeting, "Come in, the kettle's boiled"

Niamh didn't say anything, but Eve caught her glancing at the four mugs on the countertop, followed by a tiny nod of approval. Her mother perched herself on a chair at the kitchen table and pointed at the garden.

"Who's the gossoon?" Gossoon was Niamh's favourite Irish word for a boy, although her mother applied it to any young man under the age of thirty.

"Luke, from the Merrion Garden Centre."

"Here to repair the fence?"

"Yes, Tom hired him - wait a sec! How did you know about my fence?" Eve knew the answer even before she asked.

"Dymphna rang Claudia, and she rang me."

"And you rang Greta, I presume."

"Sure, why wouldn't I? Isn't it nice the girls are all interested in you, and worry about you?"

The "girls" were all in their early eighties, and weren't so much interested as deeply and incurably nosey. But it was nice to know they cared, Eve admitted to herself. Out loud she just snorted and pushed the plate towards her mother.

"Here, dig in before the men scoff them all."

"Have you no cake?" Niamh complained. "I was looking forward to a nice slice of madeira or a scone."

"If I'd known you were coming," Eve said pointedly, "I would have bought some."

"I thought you *did* know," Niamh said slyly. "Never mind. Dymphna is sure to bring some."

"Why would she bring some?"

"Because I invited her to meet me here, for a cup of tea, of course. Keep up, Eve. Honestly, sometimes you're as distracted. Artistic temperament, I suppose."

"Mam. I have to go to work - I have a class this afternoon." Eve tried not to show how exasperated she was. "Can't you go visit Dymphna in her house? Like, it's right next door…"

"Of course I could, don't be silly. But I wanted to see you too. Honestly, you don't think sometimes. Anyway, you go to your class, I'll stay here with Dymphna and make sure the boys don't mess up your garden." She peered through the window and grinned. "God, he's a nice looking young fella, isn't he?"

"Luke?" Eve looked at her mother in consternation.

"What?" her mother said. "Oh, no, he's far too young, love. You couldn't date a lad his age. Well, you could - but I wouldn't advise it. After your Dad died, I had a dalliance …but, that's not here nor there. Just take my word for it, it isn't a good idea. No, I meant Tom of course. Now, there's a suitable young man for you. I wish the pair of ye would move things on. You're not getting any younger, you know."

Her head reeling, Eve tucked away Niamh's half-revelation of a romantic entanglement with a young man in the recesses of her mind, to be taken out and looked at some other time. Perhaps, never.

"Mam, leave Tom alone. We're very happy, and we are - we are moving at our own speed. Now, make them a cup of tea when they're ready. I'm going to my class."

"Off with you. But remember, faint heart ne'er won the sprightly gardener." Niamh winked at her and stuffed a Jaffa cake into her mouth.

Eve withdrew, with what dignity she could master. Honestly, almost fifty one years of age, and still her mother could make her feel like an awkward teenager. She stomped down the main road towards the Community Centre, her mood not improved by the realization that she had left without saying goodbye to Tom - and him doing her such a big favour. Blast her mother and the whole interfering wagon load of old biddies.

Luckily for Eve, it was hard to remain in a bad mood when her class was in such great form. Her four teenagers, still in school uniform under their aprons, had come directly from St. Ignatius Secondary. Her six retirees were eager to get started, her class being the highlight of the day for many of them. Not for the first time, she thought perhaps she should do more than just teach art - perhaps, with Christmas coming, she should organize some social event for the class. Another thing to add to the list, she told herself. But this one was a bit more important than buying fancy soap for Mairead's room…she really wanted to reward the students for their commitment.

By the time they had worked on their current projects - Eve had introduced them to abstract art during the last month or so, and was enjoying the reaction - she had forgiven Niamh: a text from Tom saying the fence was finished and he would hang on to see her when she got home, if that was okay, brought a smile to her face.

"Ooh, Miss. Who's texting ya?" Barny, a seventy year old retired bus driver asked with a cheeky grin.

"You're worse than the teens, Barny," she pointed out.

"We wouldn't ask you such a personal question, Miss." Jenny Chan shook her head at Barny. "You should just nick her phone, and read it when she's not looking. She's always leaving it unlocked."

The class roared with laughter, including Eve.

"You're all a bunch of cheeky gits," she rebuked them mildly. "Okay, I think that's it for today. I wonder, would ye be interested in having a bit of a Christmas celebration, maybe closer to the day?"

Excited agreement rippled though the group.

"Where, though?" Barny asked

"I'm not sure, leave it with me. Maybe a Friday afternoon… Jenny, Pierce, Malachy and Jakob, you'll need to get permission from your parents."

Jenny laughed. "Who will Barny have to get permission from?"

"His wife!" Fiona, a retired nurse, pointed at Barny. "He's well under the thumb. He's only allowed here because there's no drink served."

"It's true," agreed Barny. "I'm a kept man, now I've given up the buses."

Eve left them cheerfully bickering. She walked quickly, eager to get home to Tom. Hopefully, Niamh and Dymphna might have retreated to Verspertilio Cottage. Her thoughts turned to possible outings for her art class. In Ireland the long Summer twilights were balanced by short December days, making it dark at five o'clock even at the beginning of the month. So lost in thought was she, she jumped and exclaimed loudly at the appearance of two hooded figures. They were standing at the point where the main road turns onto Bramble Lane, half hidden by shrubbery. The street lights were too widely spaced to cover the area, and all in all, they struck Eve as both suspicious and threatening.

Until she realized that they were only teenagers, of an age with her younger art students - sixteen year olds, at a guess. They were dressed in the ubiquitous uniform of young Dubliners, dark coloured hoodies over matching tracksuit bottoms and brightly coloured sneakers. As her eyes took in their size and youth, she felt her fright recede. It was helped by the fact that the pair had their hands full, with armfuls of what looked like straw.

"Sorry!" both exclaimed, looking so contrite the last of Eve's fear vanished.

"No, it's all right. I'm sorry. You just gave me a fright. It's so dark here…" Eve finished weakly, knowing she had reacted unfairly to a pair of kids.

"It's very dark here." The taller of the pair smiled at her shyly, a girl with large brown eyes, a shock of hair so red it was visible even in the poor light, and a friendly, open face.

"We were lurking," offered her companion, a slightly younger boy with similar eyes, hair almost as red and a thin, clever face.

Eve laughed. "You were, a bit. But I wasn't looking where I was going. No harm done." She glanced at the armfuls of straw. "Do you live around here?"

"Um. Yes. Off the main road. In the houses that back onto the meadow."

Eve blinked at the description of the wasteland, with its undergrowth of brambles bordering a field of weeds, as a "meadow" but nodded. "And, do you mind me asking, is that…straw?"

There was complete silence for a long moment.

"School. It's for school. For…a nativity play." The boy elbowed the girl. "Isn't it?"

"Yes. Anyway, sorry for the fright. We have to get home."

"Of course." Eve smiled at the pair. "Well, it was nice to meet you. Hope the play goes well."

She watched them make their way out onto the main road, and turn in the direction of the main Merrion road.

"It was plausible," she thought. "So, why do I feel like they were lying to me?"

Her mother would say, listen to your instincts.

Chapter 3

Eve's phone pinged, interrupting her flow as she added the final touches to her commissioned paintings. She tutted impatiently, wiping her hands on her paint rag. Niamh and Dymphna had settled in to her kitchen for a big chat the previous evening, only leaving when Eve had pointedly opened the front door and ordered them out. She had only managed a few minutes chat with Tom, who understandably beat a retreat in the face of two giggling octogenarians. A restless night's sleep had followed and now, just as she was getting somewhere with her work, her phone interrupted her.

"Should have put it on silent," she grumbled, but she looked anyway.

"New neighbours! Moving in RIGHT NOW!"

Margaret Fury, the young teacher who lived in Wisteria Cottage, had sent a round robin text to all the Bramble Lane residents. Eve gave a little squeal of excitement and ran to her window. It wasn't that long since she had moved in herself, and she remembered the mix of happiness, nerves and stress. Peering through the old fashioned lace curtains that had somehow made their way on to her windows - thanks to her mother, in fact - she could see a large moving truck with "Happy Homes House Moves," emblazoned on the side, parked outside what used to be known as O'Reilly's.

"Holly Cottage, now," Eve muttered. "Well, I suppose I should go say hello."

She did a quick rummage in her kitchen cupboards. Because of her mother's frequent raids on her supply of biscuits and cakes, she had taken to hiding a few goodies around the place. And, as she had admitted to Dymphna, it stopped her grazing on them too. There was a rather nice chocolate biscuit cake from a local bakery, carefully wrapped up in a tin. She grabbed a few plastic plates and hastily cut slices - when she had moved in, it had taken her ages to find her crockery and a slice of cake would have gone down nicely.

"Great minds," remarked Margaret with a grin, as Eve approached. The school teacher was standing in the driveway of Holly Cottage, with Tom, Dymphna and a sheepish looking Ronan. He was in his usual work gear of dark, well cut suit and heavy overcoat and looked as if he was there under duress. The others all clutched plates, laden with a mixture of cakes, biscuits and in Dymphna's case, slices of her famous Barm Brack. Most people baked the tea brack at Halloween, but Dymphna had made a specialty of it, all year round.

"Ah. So, we all came prepared."

"They won't have to buy anything nice for a week," Ronan said. "Look, are we going to introduce ourselves or what? I'm sorry, but I have to get back to work. I only popped home to get lunch."

"Hush, love. We'll only be a few minutes," Margaret said. "And you know you're as curious as the rest of us. You almost fell out the window trying to catch a glimpse of them."

Ronan's cheeks went pink, but he managed a dignified sniff.

"Leave him alone, Margaret," Eve said. "He can't help it,

it's his training. You don't get to be a top detective, without developing a healthy interest in other people's business."

"Thanks - I think!" Ronan's smile softened the rather stern lines of his face, and he winked at Margaret. "I won't tell them how long you've been standing in your driveway today, just so you could "accidentally," bump into the Marrinans."

It was Margaret's turn to blush. "Anyway, we're all here now. They've been in and out to the van for the last hour, I think they're taking a break. We could ring the doorbell and just say hi, and leave the plates."

They all trooped up to the front door, Eve noting that it had already been painted a bright, Christmas red. The O'Reilly's had harboured notions, trying to turn the old cottage into a modern urban home. Beige had featured heavily, along with very expensive shades of off-white and muted pastels. The red suited the place better, against bright newly painted white walls, and with the window frames and sills picked out in the same rich colour as the door.

Dymphna rang the doorbell firmly, and they could hear it echo shrilly inside the house. Someone called out, "Just a minute!" and the door opened, revealing a burly man, in brown overalls.

"Not me," His voice was deep and two bright blue eyes twinkled in a tanned, lined face. "I'm just the moving man. You'll want the lady of the house."

On cue, a mop of dark curly hair popped up behind his shoulder. "I'm here, Noel. Thank you."

Noel gave them a parting smile, cast a longing look at the plates of food and lumbered down the hallway, disappearing into the living room. The owner of the unruly curls, an attractive woman in her mid-forties, looked a little taken aback as she regarded the neighbourhood delegation, but she rallied well.

"Hi," She said brightly. "I'm Ellen Marrinan. How can I help you?"

Her accent held a slight twang of American but was unmistakably Kilkenny in origin.

"Ellen, my name is Dymphna Moriarty. This is Eve Caulton, Margaret Fury, Ronan Desmond and Tom MacDonagh. We're your neighbours."

She thrust her plate of Barm Brack at the woman. "We know you're mad busy, so we won't impose. Unless you need a hand, in which case I volunteer Tom and Ronan."

Ronan let out a tiny yelp of annoyance, but a cold eye from Dymphna silenced him.

"Anyway," she smiled graciously at Ellen, "I'm sure you'll need a break at some point, so we've brought a few bits and pieces. Have them with a cup of tea."

Eve remembered her plastic plates.

"Oh, in case you can't find your plates and stuff, I brought these over."

"Oh." Ellen seemed a little overwhelmed. "Wow. That's really kind, I appreciate it. I would love to invite you all in, but we're in a bit of a state. We've managed to move in some boxes but there's so little space, we need to unpack them before we can get the next lot in…"

"No, we're the ones disturbing you. We couldn't let you move in without saying hello, but we'll be off now." Dymphna ushered the others back a few steps. "I'm Verspertilio, Eve here is Kimberly. Tom lives at Rowan Tree House, Ronan is Copper Beech and Margaret is Wisteria. You'll get it straight after a while, don't worry."

"I suppose, we're Holly Cottage!" Ellen smiled, revealing two dimples. "Please do call around again, when we're settled. We would love to meet you all properly."

A man's voice, with a strong American accent, called from the living room, "Ellen! We found the box of bed linen!"

"That's my husband, Finn. I'd better get back to it. Thanks for all this," she nodded at her armful of plates and cake tins. "Lovely."

The neighbours made their way out of the driveway, pausing when they'd reached a decent distance for a postmortem.

"Very nice," opined Margaret.

"She does seem nice,"Eve agreed. "Very friendly, and I think once they're settled in, they'll be sociable."

In recent months, it had become very important to Bramble Lane that they were all on good terms. Even the once reclusive Ronan Desmond had become part of the social life of the street. With Christmas coming, it was something to look forward to - evenings in each other's houses, dinner parties, calling around to sample baking and compare decorations.
"I loved her hair," Eve added, "Lovely curls, so natural."
The general consensus was that the newcomers were all they had hoped, although of course they hadn't met the rest of the family yet. But with a nice mother like that, how bad could the kids and husband be?

After lunch, Eve got stuck into her work again, and to her relief, found herself contemplating a finished painting. The client had supplied a photo of her husband's favourite beach in Kerry, the beautiful Rossbeigh beach, a mile or so from Glenbeigh. She had enclosed a note saying that the man was now too ill to visit the area, where they had spent many happy summers, and could Eve recreate the scene in a painting? Eve had jumped at the chance, having visited the strand many times. Now, as she held it up to the wintry daylight streaming in her front window, she felt a stab of pride in a job well done, the painting she had created a shimmering sunset reflected in the wet sand, the sun breaking through clouds to illuminate the long shore, and the mountains of the Dingle peninsula behind.

Her happy moment was shattered by the sound of angry voices. Glancing out the window, she saw a young man, perhaps sixteen years old, but well-built and broad for his age, striding past her gate. A voice she recognized as Finn Marrinan's bellowed after him - "Come back here, right now."

The boy turned and made a rude gesture, then shouted back, "You dragged me here, to this dump, and now you won't even let me go explore it!"

A tall, broad-shouldered man appeared at her gate. He bore enough resemblance to the boy for Eve to guess they were father and son. He had a shock of dark hair, like his wife, but unlike her pale delicate features, he had a round face with a ruddy complexion. Or perhaps he was just red in the face with anger, Eve reflected. She would have been incandescent with rage if either of her kids had behaved like that, especially in public.

She peered at the teenager. His face was as red as his father's but he had an air of misery that tugged at her heartstrings. She wasn't able to see from this distance but she was willing to bet the boy was choking back tears.

Finn lowered his voice but even his quiet voice sounded loud and carried far in the quiet suburban cul de sac.

"Boyd, you need to calm down. Your mother is up to her eyes, trying to sort everything out. You can't just storm out and leave everything to us and Melly."

Boyd and Melly, Eve thought, must be the kids' names. Unusual, although not outlandish by today's standards. Only the previous week, some internet celebrity had named their baby Bookcase, which seemed awful until you realized their first kid had been called Spot. Liam had sent her a screenshot of the article, with a row of laughing emojis and the caption, "Imagine being called after the dog!"

And Boyd, she thought, what a coincidence. That was her mother's maiden name. Her Grandfather had been a Boyd. It made a rather nice first name, and she felt an immediate connection to the young lad.

"You don't need me, Dad. You like to arrange everything without even asking us. And now you've let that snake follow us here - what the hell were you thinking?"

"Son, come back inside. Please. We'll explain…"

Boyd didn't answer his dad, just shook his head sadly, turned on his heel and mooched off. Finn stood staring after him, his face impassive but a defeated slump to his shoulders.

All was not well in Holly Cottage, Eve thought.

All was not well elsewhere, as it soon transpired. A text from Claudia Warren, one of her mother's close friends, she of the Irish Women's Brigade, made Eve stop in her tracks.

Eve, what will we do about the field at the back of Bramble lane?

The trouble with Niamh's age group, she thought wearily, was that they assumed everyone just knew what they were on about, no matter how obscure or out of left field the subject was.

"The field? What about it?

The reply came so quickly, Claudia must have been typing it before she asked.

"Sold to some greedy developer. Planning on ripping it up and building on it."

Eve stared at the screen in dismay.

The large field, bordered by scrub and brambles and tangled undergrowth was something they all took for granted. It gave the illusion of living in a rural area, in the heart of a city suburb. That it survived this long, without being built on, in a city constantly in need of fresh housing was a minor miracle. If she had stopped to think about it, she would have admitted that sooner or later the inexorable march of progress would have claimed it - but to this moment, it had never occurred to her.

A new housing estate, right behind Bramble lane - between them and the houses that lined the main Merrion road. Or worse, maybe a large factory or an apartment block, overshadowing them.

She typed back quickly,

"Are you sure? Where did you hear it?"

It was always possible that Claudia had got hold of the wrong end of the stick. She was as sharp as a tack but the Irish Women's Brigade was a whirlpool of gossip at the best of times. Maybe she had picked something up wrong.

The reply came back quickly.

"Gráinne Pearse, husband architect Graham Pearse. He's been hired, development of 10 luxury houses. Luxury, my foot. Overpriced, cramped boxes."

Eve sighed. There was no denying the city needed more housing, but affordable homes - not more "luxury builds." The demand to live in areas that were considered desirable meant that people would pay through the nose for badly built, cramped houses as long as the postcode was right.

If it had been a development of affordable housing - well, it would have lessened the sting. Maybe it would be nice to have young families nearby, growing up in houses in a nice, well serviced area. But just another round of over-priced homes, that was hard to swallow. And more traffic, more pressure on local amenities.

At least it was housing, not a shopping centre or factory. She wandered out into the back garden and stood at her newly mended fence, looking over the expanse of green beyond. All those wild plants and flowers, bulldozed under. She felt bereft, not least because she had never fully appreciated the space before this.

Her phone pinged again, the WhatsApp group for the Bramble Lane residents this time. Claudia had been busy - while not actually a resident of Bramble Lane, she did live nearby, and she and her friends had become fixtures in all their lives now. She had obviously tipped off Dymphna too, and Dymphna was raging, if her messages were anything to go by. Three scalding rants in quick succession. Eve's eyebrows raised as she read them - she hadn't realized that her neighbour even knew some of those words.

Tom had responded in a more reasonable tone, voicing the same reaction as Eve.

"I wouldn't mind if it was affordable housing but we don't need more overpriced homes."

And Margaret had chimed in with -

"Even that isn't suitable for that space. Environmental disaster - that field is home to local wildlife, plants. They can't just tear it up!"

Eve thought for a moment and then opened a new group chat, including Niamh, Claudia and the infamous Greta Goode along with the Bramble Lane residents. She couldn't add in the Marrinans yet, but as soon as she got their phone numbers she would rectify that.

"Hi everyone! Let's put our heads together and see if we can do anything about this new estate. We could at least try to save some of the green space, the hedgerows etc. If we can contact the property developers, and find out what exactly is planned, better than panicking and speculation."

She half-expected a rebuff from the older ladies at least; they were used to giving orders rather than taking suggestions. But the first to respond was Dymphna with a resounding yes.

"Good girl, yes, we are flapping around. Let's get together and make a plan. Meet tonight, if possible?"

Ronan, who had been conspicuously silent until now, finally responded.

"Awkward for me. Agree in principle, definitely. Will talk later."

Of course, as a Garda Detective it wasn't really the done thing to be involved in a protest, however mild and well-mannered, Eve acknowledged. But as a private citizen and local resident, Ronan was entitled to an opinion and he could help once it didn't clash with his duties. And it was reassuring to know the level-headed, calm Garda agreed with them, this was not a good development.

One by one, the others responded. Niamh, like Margaret, was concerned about the environmental impact.

"Just what we need, more cars and another green space destroyed!"

Claudia promised to gather what intel she could from her friend, the architect's wife. The last word went to Greta Goode.

"That space was earmarked for local amenities - park, playground etc not housing. Backhanders! Brown Paper Envelopes! I'll get digging."

In the recent past, Ireland's great and powerful had been known to take some added incentives in the way of cash stuffed into *brown paper envelopes* - a phrase that now symbolized backhanders and corruption of all kind. Eve doubted there was really any such skulduggery at play - in the current housing crisis, any plan to build homes was attractive to the County Council, and land was rezoned and repurposed all the time. But if anyone could ferret out the details, it was Greta and her loyal followers, the Goode Hunters. Her podcast - Greta's Gory Truths - was more popular than ever but the original hardcore fans had their own, private chat forums that Greta could utilize discreetly.

She sighed. All this had taken the gloss off her holiday preparations. But then again, no point worrying until they knew for sure what they were dealing with - and in the end, they would just have to put up with whatever came their way. After all, how bad could it be?

Chapter 4

"It's a hideous eyesore," Dymphna fumed, her face a picture of outrage. "And they will have to cut down every tree and every bit of the hedgerow, just to squeeze in that many houses!"

Claudia had outdone herself. Her friend Gráinne had supplied a photo of the proposal, complete with a fancy mock-up of the completed new housing estate. Each house was, to Eve's artistic eye, a monument to bad taste. Mock Tudor designs, with fake wood and paneled glass, vied with imitation Georgian classical columns and even an attempt at Victorian Gothic.

The proposal boasted that the estate would offer "individuality."

The residents had convened in Dymphna's, who had volunteered to host. They sat transfixed by the images on Claudia's laptop, staring in a kind of fascinated horror.

"They're certainly...*unique.*" Margaret said. "Goodness, how many different styles are there? Oh - there's one that looks like a doll's house...pink, with a sort of striped awning..."

"It really doesn't matter what they look like - although, they *are* hideous. What's important is how it's going to affect the area, what damage will be done to the environment, and so on," Ronan warned. "And are we just being...well, selfish?"

"I know what you mean," Eve nodded. "Are we just reluctant to have our view spoiled? Or are we right to be concerned?"

The newspapers had long ago coined the phrase "Nimbies," for just this situation. The acronym, NIMBY, stood for "Not in my back yard," for all those times people objected to anything in their area that benefited other people. Especially people they felt didn't "belong" in that area.

"Can we be Nimbies if we're objecting to rich people?" Tom grinned.

"I don't know. I do think I'd feel better about this whole scheme if the houses would benefit people who actually need houses, rather than just those who want a posh postcode." Eve looked around the front room of Margaret Fury's cottage. "I remember the absolute relief I felt when I was able to buy Kimberly. It was beyond my wildest dreams. Even with half the sale of my old house, I genuinely feared I would end up in some brutal apartment block out on the motorway. It was all I could - barely - afford. I wouldn't begrudge that to anyone else."

Dymphna rolled her eyes.
"Ah here, we'd all be fine if it was in a good cause - although frankly I'd still fight them to ensure enough green space remained. Every development should have an area for kids to play, and people to walk their dogs. This whole plan here - all this excess, all these ugly houses - it's a vanity project, and a way to part gullible people from their cash."

Eve didn't bother arguing; her friend came from a generation that had known poverty and hardship but had worked their way through it. Dymphna would never understand people spending money just to have a nice address. It wasn't a vanity she particularly understood herself, either.

Margaret produced a large book, entitled "Flora and Fauna of Ireland," by Professor Eithne Blennerville. It was an impressive tome, hardback with a glossy dustsheet cover, featuring pictures of various plants and animals.

"I did some digging," she announced proudly. "One of my colleagues is big into environmental issues. This is the book they use, to identify any rare animal or plant that might halt construction. She's hoping to get someone to come over the weekend and survey the field, see what's there."

"Margaret, that's inspired!" Tom gave her a thumbs up. She blushed, looking delighted.

"I was thinking," Niamh offered, "What if there's some archaeology or history associated with the site? That might be worth pursuing."

Claudia started writing down bullet points on a large A4 pad. "Good. I was thinking myself, there must be some reason why they never built on the field until now. What if there's a stream underground or something like that? They built on an underground stream over in Harold's Cross and one day all the gardens collapsed, total mess."

There was another murmur of approval from the group at this suggestion.

"Any other ideas? I was wondering - oh, that's the doorbell." Dymphna stood up, brushing crumbs from her long, dark skirt. She dressed in a way that while perfectly modern, did remind Eve of a Victorian matron. "I dropped a note in the Marrinans' letterbox, it might be Ellen or Finn."

She disappeared into the hall, and within minutes, ushered Ellen Marrinan into the living room. "Here she is!"

A chorus of greeting rumbled around the room. Ellen raised a hand, shyly, and waved in response. Eve thought she looked uncomfortable, maybe the new neighbour wasn't as outgoing or extrovert as they had thought. It probably was a bit daunting to walk into a close knit group of neighbours, especially when feelings were running so high.

She patted the one empty place on the sofa and smiled reassuringly. "Sit down, and we'll fill you in. We're all a bit concerned about the news - have you heard? About the development."

Ellen didn't budge from where she was standing, despite Eve's invitation. She just nodded slightly. Eve frowned, and caught Tom's eye.

"We thought - I know, you've only just moved in, but you're part of us now." Tom grinned. "And that field is the only large green space in this area, apart from the golf course. I know it's been under utilized but for years the council promised us a small park with a playground. It's a terrible pity to see it become just another housing estate…"

He trailed off, in the face of Ellen's silence. The atmosphere was becoming decidedly uncomfortable.

Greta stood and extended her hand. "I'm Greta, a friend of Eve's. I live nearby, we all do. Consider us the extended resident's committee." Ellen stared at the outstretched hand but didn't take it.

The room fell silent.

With a sudden intake of breath, Ellen finally spoke.

"I'm so sorry. I really am. But - you don't understand. I was so upset when I got Mrs. Moriarty's note about the meeting. It never occurred to us, either of us, that you would be upset by the development. We've been told over and over about the need for additional housing, and that the country is crying out for more homes, and - oh dear!"

Eve stared at the woman, bewildered, until the penny finally dropped.

"Finn. He's a property developer, in the States." She blurted it out without thinking.

Ellen nodded again. "Yeah. It's our business. We bought the field from the council, they can't develop it due to budget cuts and…long story short, we're the ones building on it."

She looked around the room, her expression a mix of defiance and embarrassment.

"So you see, I can't possibly join the residents' protest. We're the ones you're protesting against."

Chapter 5

Eve set down her almost untouched cup of tea, and sighed.

"Well, that was an unmitigated disaster."

Everyone except Claudia and Niamh had left Verspertilio Cottage. Ellen had left the moment she delivered her bombshell, leaving the others to a shell-shocked discussion of this new turn of events. Eve felt miserable. Their happy little community was divided, with a new family pitted against the older residents. It was a most unpleasant feeling.

"Cheer up,"Dymphna fluttered around her small kitchen, tidying away the debris from the evening's gathering. "At least she was honest - imagine if we had sat there revealing all our plans only to find out we were on opposite sides!"

"What happens now?" Eve wondered. The two older women exchanged glances.

"What do you think?" Claudia snorted. "We fight them tooth and nail. Well, obviously I don't live right beside it - but as a local resident, I am involved. And I say no way should we let this happen."

"Even if they altered the plans," Dymphna added, "Fewer houses, and more green space, build the playground the council promised…"

Eve thought of the boy and girl she had bumped into earlier

that week, not to mention the teenagers in her art class. "The local kids haven't that much to do, do they? Unless they get the dart out towards Blackrock, or trek into town. The younger kids could use a playground and the older ones need some kind of focus too. The community centre does its bit but other places have skate parks and outdoor gym equipment."

"You know what annoys me?" Claudia stood with her hands on her hips, looking every inch the Brigadier General of the Irish Women's Brigade. "We all know this, we all knew the council had reneged on building a playground, and we did absolutely nothing about it til it was too late."

"It's not too late yet," Dymphna smiled. "Finn Marrinan doesn't know yet what he's up against. We'll sort this out - by hook or by crook!"

This did little to alleviate Eve's sense of unease. Dymphna - while by and large a benevolent force - was capable of quite a lot of mischief if provoked. In fact, Niamh and Claudia were equally formidable, and that was without taking the irrepressible Greta into account. It wasn't just that they might chain themselves to the railings, and climb trees - although she wouldn't put it past them - but they were equipped with very special skills, honed over generations of practice and tradition. In short, Finn and Ellen might find themselves the target of a bunch of angry wise women, dedicated to making their lives unpleasant in a thousand tiny ways. Or one or two spectacular ways, depending on their mood.

"Promise me, the lot of you - and you can tell Greta this too -promise me you'll exhaust mundane methods before you do anything…anything extra."

Dymphna rolled her eyes. "Oh my God, Eve, when will you stop being so afraid of your own heritage? Your mother here, she is one of the most talented women I've ever known. Claudia and Greta have dedicated their lives to the old ways, to our folk magic and our traditions. I'm not one for self praise, but I know my own ability. You have as much talent, if only you'd stop pussyfooting about."

"Eve *has* been practicing, in fairness. And she isn't half as silly about it as she used to be." Niamh said loyally. "But Dymphna is right, Eve. If we don't know by now when to use magic and when not to, it'd be a disgrace."

"I know ye." Eve stuck to her guns. "You say *now* you won't interfere, you'll be patient, you'll wait and see how normal methods work for us. Then one of you will get bored, and next thing we know the Marrinans are dealing with a plague of frogs and their car keys keep going missing."

"That's absolute nonsense," Claudia sniffed. "That frog thing was completely exaggerated and anyway, he richly deserved it."

"My point is, you all need to calm down and do this the simple way. We look into the history and environment angles, we write to local politicians, we get the rest of the local residents involved. No extreme measures."

Niamh grinned. "Nothing extreme, that's fair enough."

Eve could almost hear the wheels turn in her neighbour's head, as she weighed what had been said and rearranged it to suit herself.

"Okay, nothing over the top," Dymphna said, "Unless they ask for it."

Claudia nodded cheerily. "Sure, we would never do anything extreme unless they deserved it, you know that. Let's just hope that normal methods yield some results. Now, ladies, I must take my leave. Early start tomorrow. Taking a bunch of youngsters to the Botanical Gardens for the Christmas Market. Need my wits about me!"

Niamh also stood. "I'd better get home too. Your brother is bringing some friend home this weekend, I've no idea who. Just left me a note saying he's a mate coming to stay on Saturday and would I please make sure the house wasn't a tip. The cheek of him. I'll talk to you all tomorrow. Good night."

Eve's brother Conor lived at home but rarely imposed on his mother, so this, in Eve's opinion was a good thing. It would keep Niamh occupied and out of trouble.

Eve waited until they left, before thanking Dymphna for hosting the meeting. She also wanted to make sure her neighbour wasn't annoyed at her.
"I'm sorry if what I said offended you, you know I think the world of you."

"Ah, get out of it. It'd take more than that to annoy me. And I'm glad to hear you've been exercising your talents - you owe it to yourself."

"I've been trying to figure out what I'm good at," Eve admitted. "It's hard."

"Follow your instincts. If it was easy, you could buy a book or watch one of those You Thingy videos. You're an artist, you see things others don't. Start there."

Eve walked the short distance back to her own house, slowly. It was a beautiful, clear night. The crisp air stung her cheeks, the stars twinkled overhead. A full bright moon illuminated the houses and cast shadows from the trees and shrubs. She smiled, despite the recent upset.

Reluctant to turn in just yet, she decided to take a stroll down the lane, to the end of the cul de sac and back. It was only nine o'clock, and while she was at it, she could call into Tom and see if he fancied some company. Or maybe she could do with an early night, it would be sensible to get an early start in the morning…as she debated with herself, she was interrupted by raised voices.

"It's typical of you!" the voice was young, with a strong American accent. The elder Marrinan child - Boyd. He sounded as if he was on the verge of tears, as well as angry.

"Boyd, come back here right now." Ellen sounded weary.

"No! You always take his side. You moved us all here, to this stupid little house, without even asking what we wanted. Now, before we've even started school or made a single friend, you've turned everyone against us. They'll all hate us now, just like at home. It's not fair!"

Finn's voice rang out. "Boyd! Come back. For the love of - you can't just walk out whenever you feel like it."
The front door opened, light spilling out from the hall and Eve instinctively shrank back into the shadows. She had no desire to eavesdrop on the Marrinan family rows - she recalled several explosive fights from Mairead's and Liam's teenage years - but the alternative was to appear in the middle of it and embarrass them all. Luckily the light only intensified the pools of darkness around the entrance to their drive.

She heard the sound of footsteps crunching on the gravel driveway, and Boyd passed by her, close enough to reach out and touch her if he had been aware that anyone was standing there. He had a hooded fleece top and a scarf, which both hid his face and blinkered him - he was probably also too upset to actually notice anyone else. He shouted, without turning his head, "Why not? You run away when things get hard. Well, I'm done running. If that woman thinks she'll destroy these people like she did in Mountain Heights, she'll find out the hard way. I'm not going to stand by and let it happen again!"

Before either of his parents could react, he was out of earshot, half walking and half running. There was a heavy sigh from Ellen Marrinan followed by a murmured, "Come back inside, Finn. The neighbours…"

After a few moments, the door shut, plunging the driveway back into darkness.

Eve shook her head. She hated any kind of row -which was probably why she had put up with Peter for so long - but it felt especially miserable to overhear a family argument. Teenagers felt things so deeply and everything was life and death, to them. It must have been a shock, to be uprooted from his home and friends and transplanted to foreign soil. Even though his mother was Irish, and Finn was second generation Irish American, it must all feel so unfamiliar. And lonely- friends were the world to you at that age, she reflected.
It put the local dispute about the housing development into perspective. Yes, saving the green space was important but here was a family, struggling to fit in in a new place. Whatever issues they had with Finn and Ellen, they shouldn't extend to the kids.

She abandoned thoughts of a walk, or of calling into Tom. Once back in the warmth of her own living room, she sat in front of her fire and thought about Boyd and Melly. There had to be ways to make them feel at home, without compromising the protest. Eve went to bed, still mulling it over.

The next day was Friday, and it dawned bright and sunny, although cold. A perfect winter's day, and the end of the working week. Eve had classes to teach that afternoon, after school hours in the local primary school hall, but the morning was free. The problem of the Marrinan children was still in her mind, and she had one idea that might extend the hand of friendship - but she needed to run it past the others.

WhatsApp groups were a great invention, she reflected. Even if Greta had already spammed the protest group with cat memes. It took only a few minutes to share her thoughts with everyone, and wait for their replies.

"Morning, all. We need to regroup after yesterday, what a bombshell! But I saw young Boyd last night, he was very upset. It's very hard on the kids, moving to a strange place and then their parents upsetting the neighbours. I want to be sure we don't make them feel unwelcome"

She pressed send, and then added, *"I was going to see if my art class students can help, the Marrinans are not in school yet so this way they can meet some local kids."*

Fingers crossed, she thought. Hopefully no one would think she was being disloyal. Not that it mattered, she reminded herself sternly, it was the right thing to do regardless of anyone else's opinion. But the habit of pleasing others was hard to break, and she had suffered years of Peter's silent sulks if she did anything he didn't fully approve of…the first reply pinged and she winced. But she need not have worried.

"Excellent idea, totally agree. I will invite them to next Brigade outing. Poor little sods, awful time of year not to be at home with your friends."

Claudia signed off every text and message, using her full name, no matter how often Niamh tried to explain to her that it wasn't necessary.

Dymphna just expected everyone to know who she was and what she was talking about.

"Agreed, there are some local events on - a Christmas crafting market in the golf club, we should make up a party and invite the

Marrinans."

Eve blinked. Invite *all* the family? She wasn't going to argue with this newfound goodwill towards the enemy, but she couldn't help wondering what her neighbour was up to. Still, reading the messages from all her friends and neighbours, all willing to embrace the younger Marrinans, she was reminded of why Bramble Lane was worth fighting for.

"And if this estate goes ahead, we'll still stick together. But I do hope Finn listens to reason." She marched off to her art class in a far better frame of mind.

The class was a combined one, open to her pupils from the midweek class as well as pupils from the primary school, some people who liked to attend on an ad-hoc basis and some who were part of the local day-time care centre for older patients. She was never sure who would be there at any time, so tried to keep the projects fun and ready to complete in an afternoon. She crossed her fingers for luck as she pushed open the doors, hoping that at least some of the young ones from St. Ignatius would be there today.

"Hello, Miss!" Jenny Chan and her shadow, the tiny and painfully shy Ciara Bailey greeted her with huge smiles.

"Hello, girls. Just the pair of you today?"

"Yes, the lads have a hurling match. But they said to tell you they'll be in Wednesday without fail."

"Great. So, how are things? School going okay?"

"Surprisingly well," Jenny grimaced. "Even the teachers are getting into the holiday spirit, which is something. Except auld Grimes, she says we'll have an exam next week and she won't even tell us what chapters to study."

"She's trying to catch us out," Ciara whispered.

"She's trying to make sure you've revised everything, more

like. I bet you're all looking forward to the break."

"Can't wait. And there's the Christmas market next week, then we're going to pick out a tree - Mam can't stand putting one up before mid December, so she made us wait! Like, everyone else has their one up by now. I bet you do, don't you, Miss? Of course you do! So we'll finally decorate the house, and a gang of us are going to busk on Grafton Street to raise money for the rough sleepers. Ciara is the soloist, aren't you?"

Ciara blushed deeply, and tried to nod and shake her head at the same time.

"Ciara, I didn't know you sang?" Eve smiled at her. "I would love to hear you. When are you doing this?"

"Saturday week. Just as everyone does last minute shopping, we'll catch them while they feel guilty about spending so much."

"I admire your cynicism, Jenny."

"I'm not a bit cynical, I'm just a businesswoman. Oh, Miss, did you hear about the new housing estate? Isn't it a disgrace? My dad has been lobbying the council for years to get a playground, since I was a kid. And I know for a fact the allotments in Booterstown begged to use it for extra space, they were planning to grow fresh fruit and veg and donate it during the pandemic. Good outdoor activity, but no. Now some rich guy owns it and it'll be an eyesore, Dad says."

He doesn't know how right he is, Eve thought. Wait til the plans are made public.

"Well, it's not built yet. We - the local residents - are planning to protest."

Jenny's face lit up. "Count us in, do! I'll round up the troops and you can rely on a good turnout. I'm president of the

Climate Crisis Club in school - I'll have the entire senior end of the school out with placards."

"I'll hold you to that. Actually, before the others arrive, can I run something past you?"

Eve gave the girls a brief synopsis of the situation, how the new neighbours were the ones planning to build on the green space and how this had affected the two younger Marrinans.

"Ah, that's a rotten situation to be in. Boyd and Melly? Okay. Maybe we could invite them to hang out - what if I call round to yours over the weekend and you can introduce us?"

Eve promised to arrange it, then the arrival of the other students prevented any further conversation. At least, she had a plan. And there was one other thing she wanted to ask Jenny, at the end of the class.

"Jenny, I met two teenagers the other night. A tall girl, with red hair and a shorter lad, possibly her brother. Same distinctive hair. They said they lived in the houses that back onto the field on the other side…"

"Ashleigh and Sean Conlan," Jenny replied promptly. "I know them, or rather my sister Kate does. She's in Sean's class. Ashleigh's in my year but - well, she keeps to herself."

"Okay thanks," Eve said. "I was just wondering."

Jenny looked at her quizzically. "She's a bit funny, Ashleigh. Sean, too. Very nice and all that, but - just a bit funny."

Eve smiled. She suspected her classmates would have described her in very similar terms, back in her teen years.

Chapter 6

Things moved quickly, far more so than Eve had expected. If there had been any sign of builders on the field in the new year, she would have considered it quick work. To find a team of men and women in hard hats already wandering around on the other side of her garden fence, with two JCBs and surveying equipment, on Saturday morning, was a shock.

The sound of engines and raised voices had disturbed her breakfast, an unwelcome intrusion into the usual peace of Bramble lane. Looking out the kitchen windows, she wasn't surprised to see Dymphna in the neighbouring garden, peering suspiciously over the fence. The workers were becoming increasingly nervous under her relentless observation, and when Eve wandered out into her own garden, one of them visibly paled. She gave them a smile that held no friendliness and was rewarded by the man, taking an involuntary step backwards. He was short, stocky and bald with a goatee beard, his yellow high viz vest marking him as "Security."

"Have you seen this," Dymphna called to her, her eyes never wavering from the huddled group of construction workers. "On a weekend, too. Don't we have laws about noise nuisance in this city?"

"We do," agreed Eve. "It's awfully early on a Saturday to be revving engines and shouting."

A tall woman, also clad in a high-viz jacket and matching yellow hard hat, looked up from a set of papers. She had a sharp, thin face and Eve guessed her age to be early fifties, like herself. But where Eve's face was youthful, with laughter lines around her eyes and a few wrinkles when she smiled, this woman had the strangely aging, smooth look of a Botox devotee.

"We were hardly making a racket," she protested. Her voice was loud, with a trace of a northern accent.

"You woke me up," Dymphna pointed out coldly. "And me an old woman. I'm eighty-two if I'm a day, and I deserve to be left in peace on a weekend. Who told you to start this on a Saturday morning?"

The woman hesitated, glancing at her companions. They studiously avoided eye contact with either her or the two women on the other side of the fence. The security man actually shuffled a few feet away.

"We have permission from the owner, and I think you'll find it's after nine a.m., which makes this a perfectly reasonable hour." She mustered a frosty smile and stepped up to the garden fence.

"I'm Dolores McIntyre. I'm the project manager for the new housing development." She spoke with an air of confidence and a dash of smugness.

Dymphna regarded her coldly. "You're loud, and inconsiderate. Why on earth were you shouting?"

"We were - um, we were measuring the space…" one of the work crew mumbled. He was a young lad, short and broad, with blond hair peeking out from under his hard hat. "So, like, we were just calling out figures to Ms. McIntyre."

Dymphna sniffed. "You couldn't write them down and then meet up quietly, then? No pens or pencils among you? No phones, you couldn't text the numbers to each other? You had no choice but to bellow them out and ruin everyone's morning?"

She drew herself up to her full height, her usual garb of black polo-neck emphasizing the severity of her expression. "Get away with yourselves. I know the owner, and he'll be hearing from me right now. Let's see how he appreciates having *his* Saturday morning ruined."

She stalked back inside her kitchen, and slammed the door. The sound echoed rather ominously. This time, everyone except Dolores backed away from the fence. Eve didn't blame them - there was a decided sense of menace lingering in the air.

Dolores seemed unmoved, however. She shrugged and addressed Eve instead.

"Look, I get it. You're all used to this being a precious little enclave, where you can all pretend to live in the countryside but with all the advantages of the city out there on the main road. But things change. This is prime real estate, and it's going to waste. Give it a year and you'll forget there was ever a field here. And when you see how much your property increases in value, you'll wonder why you ever objected."

She gave a short laugh. "I've seen it time and time again. You all belly-ache until you figure out that it's actually to your benefit."

"I beg your pardon," Eve was damned if she was going to be lectured by a complete stranger. "Property prices are not the be all and end all of life, you know. We want something on that field that benefits everyone in the community, not just a lucky few, rich enough to buy overpriced houses. And that land was public land until recently, don't you forget that."

She glared at the other workers. "None of you should be here." The men had the grace to look embarrassed, and even Dolores was quiet.

Once safely inside her own kitchen again, with the door firmly closed, she wished she had been able to think of a stronger comeback - but at least she had spoken up. Even a few years earlier, she would have remained silent and fumed internally. It was a little exciting, she had to admit. And while she found it hard to dislike Ellen, or even Finn, Dolores was another matter. Rude, patronizing woman.

She and Dymphna weren't the only ones whose mornings had been disrupted by the builders. Tom called in with croissants from the bakery in the nearby shopping centre, citing the early noise as an excuse.
"I figured we could use a little treat after that start to the day." He winked at her. "If you had some jam and real butter, I wouldn't tell anyone."

Over tea and croissants, they avoided any mention of the protest or strife among the neighbourhood but once she had cleared the tea things away, Tom drummed his fingers on the wooden table and sighed.

"Tell me about young Boyd."

She explained how it came about that she had overheard the second row between Boyd and his parents that week.

"Honestly I felt so trapped, if I moved they'd have known I heard them and if I stayed hidden, I was eavesdropping."

"Ah, you did the right thing. It wasn't your fault, sure any of us could have been outside and overheard. That's the problem with having shouting matches on your doorstep."

"Teenagers are hard, Tom." Tom was a widower, who had never had children. "You never imagine your sweet little kid will grow into a hulking great sixteen year old, who thinks you're thick, and who feels like the whole world is against them. But it happens."

"I'll take your word for it. But your two turned out just fine, don't you think? I'm sure Boyd will settle in, the poor lad. What he needs are some mates in the area."

"Ah. I have a plan for that."

Eve explained about Jenny and the gang from St Ignatius. "Jenny said she would call over if I text her, and she'll invite Boyd and Melly out to hang with them."

"She can't just knock on the door and say, "Howya, is Boyd in? He doesn't know me but I'm here to make friends."" Tom objected. "That's not going to go down well with any teenager."

"You haven't met Jenny," Eve chuckled. "She is perfectly capable of that, and more. But it's up to me to engineer a meeting, and that's where I'm stuck."

"You leave that to me. Text young Jenny and ask her to be here in about an hour."

Jenny countered with an offer to be there in an hour and half.

"Mam has me cleaning my room, she's obsessed with tidying. I blame that Marie Kondo one, with her minimalism. I'll be there straight after, though."

One problem solved, Eve thought. Next on the agenda was moving up this protest. If Finn could get the builders in so quickly, they were going to have to match him. She fired up her laptop and googled for any local newspapers and radio stations. Within half an hour, she had a list of four Dublin newspapers, and two community radio stations. National media might be important too, but she wasn't sure that she could compose a professional enough press release to catch their interest. Starting locally seemed a lot less daunting.

It took her a while to put together a letter that explained the situation and provided details of the proposed build - without betraying Gráinne Pearse's kindness in supplying the details to her Brigadier. She added in some pictures that showed off the green area in a good light, and having found a link to an article from several years prior that announced plans for a playground and park on the space, added that in for good measure. Just before pressing send, she thought for a moment. There was no harm in providing a bit of good luck, to help it on its way.

She searched the back of her pantry. Earlier in the autumn she had collected some Rowan berries, and made a paste of them. Mixed in with bits of rowan twigs and leaves, it made a very effective protective spell, used correctly. It wasn't much good for an email, unless she smeared it across the screen, but there was something with it that might help. Her fingers closed on the jar, and she pulled it out triumphantly. There, on the little dark green jar, was a hand-painted label. She had painted it quickly, while standing under the Rowan tree that had given Tom's cottage its name.

"I knew there was a reason I painted you," she grinned. It was the work of a minute to snap a photo on her phone, upload it to her computer and crop it so that the rowan tree painting formed a neat little image. She attached this to her email, for added luck, and pressed "send."

A knock at the door reminded her that she was expecting company. Jenny bounced in, with Ciara and the boys from the class in tow. Mikey, a tough looking boy with a spikey haircut

- who was as gentle as a lamb - and Darren who was slight, and pale and a black belt in Taekwando .

"Well, I wasn't expecting all of you. But you're all welcome. Tom wants us to go to his house, he has a plan for getting the Marrinans to meet you."

Jenny led the way, the others trooping behind. Eve couldn't help but laugh as the young girl bossed the others around in a cheerful way. She was a natural leader, with more than a hint of Claudia's firmness. If the Brigadier ever met the girl, she would recruit her on sight.

Tom waved at them, from his front garden. He had moved his car out of the driveway and in its place was a stack of tightly packed bags, each bearing the label, "Merrion Garden Centre." "Ah, reinforcements!" He gestured at the bags, speaking in what Eve considered his "amateur dramatics" voice. It was designed to be clear, and carrying. "I need to get this bark down, before the weather breaks. I hope you're here to give me a hand?"

Jenny caught on faster than Eve. She had the advantage of being able to see the road from where she stood.

"Oh hello, Mr. MacDonagh. Yeah, sure, we'll help. Those bags are heavy though, aren't they?" She gave one an experimental shove and winced. "If we take one end each, maybe we can lift it down..."

Casting a glance at the roadside, she added loudly, "Don't attempt to lift it, Mikey, not with your bad arm."

Mikey blinked in surprise, his mouth opening, but a well aimed elbow in the ribs from Ciara silenced him.

"Yeah," Ciara said pointedly, "The hurling team would go mad if you make it worse. You don't want to set your recovery back."

Mikey eyed her with a bewildered air. "My arm?"

"Yeah. Your bad arm." She poked him in the ribs and rolled her eyes. The penny finally dropped.

"Oh. Yeah. Sorry - I can't risk hurting my arm again. I'd be happy to help otherwise."

Eve risked looking in the direction of the gate. Jenny's eagle eyes had spotted her quarry, Boyd Marrinan, standing quietly by the gate. Beside him was a young girl, with the same black curls as her mother, peeking around his shoulder.

"That must be Melly," Eve thought. It was the first time she had seen the child, but there was no mistaking her resemblance to Ellen.

Young Darren took up the thread. "I'll do my bit, Jenny, but it would be easier if we'd another pair of hands. Ah well."

Jenny bent as if to lift one of the heavy bags of ornamental bark and Boyd stepped forward, saying sharply, "Don't do that! You'll wreck your back."

He strode over and lifted one easily, turning to Tom and asking, "Where do you need it?" His sister slipped in behind him, offering a nervous smile to the other girls.

"Oh, over here, near that flower bed. Thank you, we could do with the help." Tom patted the lad on the shoulder and handed a small shovel to Jenny. "If you hold the bag and Jenny spreads the bark, that'd work."

Melly looked a little dismayed at being left alone with a bunch of strangers while Boyd followed Jenny to the furthest bed, against the boundary wall. Ciara grinned at her.

"I'm Ciara, this is Darren and that big lump is Mikey. Are you on for helping? We could get that bag over to the wall and start spreading the bark on that bed…"

"I'm Melly," she said, in a soft voice. "Short for Amelia. Yeah, sure. I'll help."

Eve retreated to the living room with Tom and left the young people to it. They watched through the window as the teens made short work of the bark spreading, laughing and chatting all the while. At one point, Mikey threw a handful of bark at Boyd, who roared and mock threatened him in return. She smiled, remembering her Liam with his friends at the same age - nothing like a good laugh to bond teenagers.

"He'll be fine," Tom said, reading her mind. "Both of them will be fine. They're a nice bunch, your students, and it'll make joining the school after the holidays so much easier."

By the time the gardening work was done, and the teenagers had a well-earned break with cake and fizzy drinks, it was clear that Tom was right. Boyd and Melly seemed to be at ease, and very much part of the group. Before she could congratulate herself on the success of her scheme, however, there was a loud knock at Tom's front door.

"Boyd? Melly?" Their father sounded both anxious and annoyed.

Tom hastened to open the door, saying, "Finn. Welcome. Boyd and Melly are here, they were kind enough to help me with a rather difficult job in my garden. They've been a godsend."

Finn appeared at the doorway to the living room, and glared at Boyd.

"I had no idea where they were," he responded rather brusquely.

"I said we were going out for an hour," Boyd said, all trace of his previous good humour eradicated.

"And I went looking for you when the hour was up. Obviously, you were nowhere to be seen." He looked at Tom and

Eve. "The young woman at whatsit-called, Wisteria Cottage, said I'd find them here."

"Yes," Tom said mildly. Eve could feel her temper rising, the man was being really quite unreasonable, but Tom looked sympathetic.

"I'm so sorry, it's my fault. I should have thought to let you know. But they worked so hard for me, and I'm really very grateful - spreading bark is an awful job to tackle on your own, which is why I didn't get to it earlier in the year. Boyd took over because Mikey here has an injury. Have you ever seen a hurling match?"

Finn blinked, trying to keep up with this rapid change of subject. "Not yet," he replied cautiously, "although Ellen has told me about it. I hear the local school has a good team."

"The best," Jenny blurted out. "I'm captain of the Camogie team - that's the women's hurling - and Mikey is one of our best male hurlers. Boyd, you should give it a go, didn't you say you used to play hockey?"

A shadow crossed the young man's face. "Yeah. I would have been on the senior team this year."

"Well, their loss might be our gain," Mikey said. "I'll get you a hurl and we'll give you a few pointers. Even just play for fun, it's a great sport. Faster than you're used to, of course."

Boyd snorted. "Hah! We'll see. You guys haven't seen an ice hockey match." But his smile was back.

Finn opened his mouth, but some shred of sense made him adopt a less confrontational tone.
"Well, that sounds pretty cool. But we'd better get home, your Mom will be wondering where everyone is." He paused and gave Tom and Eve an awkward wave. "So, yeah, thanks. Nice to meet you both."

He ushered out his children, closing the door behind them. Jenny rolled her eyes. "Wow. Sure, he nearly accused us of kidnapping them!"

Eve was inclined to agree but Tom shook his head. "Two unhappy teens, in a strange city, wandering around - of course, he was worried. He's just being a good dad."

"I like Boyd," Darren remarked. "Melly too."

"Yeah, they're grand," Mikey agreed. "I promised we'd all hook up again tomorrow. I'll add them to the group chat."

Jenny winked at Eve. "Problem solved, eh?"

Eve nodded, but didn't like to point out, that was only one of their problems out of the way.

Chapter 7

By the following Wednesday, when time for Eve's mid-week art class rolled around, there had been quite a lot of developments. Jenny and her gang seemed to have seamlessly incorporated the Marrinans into their fold; it had become quite a familiar sight to see the group wandering around Bramble Lane, or to pass them in the Merrion Centre. And Jenny had thrown herself, and her school's environmental studies group, into the campaign to save the green space.

"There are builders, surveyors, and more equipment there every day now," she complained to Eve. "If we don't act soon it'll be too late."

Claudia Warren, as predicted by Eve, was most impressed with the girl.

"Brigade material, if ever I saw it," she announced. "And she's right, it's time we stopped faffing around. Action is required."

And now action was in motion. Eve set her class to the unscheduled, but very popular task of creating protest signs. The older members were ready to fight for the cause and proudly displayed their slogans. "Community Comes First," said one, and "No one asked what WE Need!" said another.

Barny the retired bus driver's poster read "Green Spaces not Posh Places," which was a compromise from the original idea he had. *That* one had been both unprintable and inflammatory, and had reduced the whole class to tears of laughter. He was reluctantly persuaded that it wasn't a good idea to libel the opposition, but it was a close run thing.

The teens concentrated on pithy environmental slogans like "Nurture Nature or Face No Future" and "Habitats for All, Not Houses for a Few."

Margaret had recruited several neighbours to conduct a survey of local residents, resulting in a comprehensive list of their misgivings and objections.

"Handy to show the press," the school teacher said. "We have the support of the majority and not just because of increased traffic and inconvenience. The consensus is that the environmental impact will be disastrous, followed by anger that it was never developed for community use, despite the promises."

Niamh and the others had less luck. There seemed to be no particular history attached to the field and no one seemed to know why on earth it had never been built on.

"We'll keep digging, but for the moment, nothing we can use."

Thursday morning at seven a.m. was the agreed kick-off moment for the active protesting. The adults who were free to do so were going to picket the site, with the younger people helping out after school or work. Ronan Desmond was chagrined that he couldn't play a more active role, but he promised to do whatever he could in other ways. True to his word, he had ferreted out every by-law and regulation that could be applied and had set Dymphna the task of recording any violations. If the builders so much as revved an engine before eight a.m. or spoke above a whisper after nine p.m., she was there with her notebook.

Eve half suspected Ronan had invented the task, to keep the old lady occupied and at the same time, unnerve the opposition. The workforce certainly seemed to dread the sight of her popping up over her fence of a morning to fix them with a beady eye.

Eve was about to turn in early on Wednesday evening, an good night's sleep seeming wise before the stress of the following day, but a sharp rap on her back door made her heart jump unpleasantly.

"Eve!" Dymphna hissed. "Open up."

Eve opened the door, her hands shaking slightly.

"For the love of - Dymphna, you put the heart crossways in me!"

"Oh, don't be silly. Sure, who else could it be?" Dymphna shook herself and flapped her arms. "I'm getting too old to be hopping over the wall. I think I'll walk."

There were people who called Dymphna an old bat, referring to her temperament. If they only knew, Eve thought.

"Walk where?"

"You'll see. The others are waiting. Bring a stepladder, you'll need it to get over the fence."

Other people have normal friends and neighbours, Eve told herself. Not ones that flutter around in the dark, or demand you clamber over garden fences into wild scrub land and thorny brambles in the middle of the night. But she put on her jacket and followed her neighbour out into the dark, because she was also one of those people.

Her eyes took a moment or two to adjust to the night. Dymphna, of course, had no such problem, weaving her way past patio furniture and plant pots with ease. Eve found out where they were when she hit her shin or ankle off them. Carrying a small folding stepladder didn't help either.

She eyed the back fence dubiously. "Even with this, I don't think I can get over there. Could we not go around and get in through the builder's entrance?"

Dymphna's voice answered from the other side of the fence, where she had quite literally, landed. "Get on with it. We'll help you down this side."

"And how will I get back over?" Eve asked. "Unless you've a ladder on your side. Thanks for waiting for me, by the way."

"Eve Caulton, will you get over yourself *and* this benighted fence!" Her mother sounded exasperated. "Claudia, Greta and I have been freezing our bums off waiting for you."

Here goes nothing, she thought. She managed to hitch herself up onto the fence, grateful that she had opted to wear a pair of fleece lined, strong tracksuit bottoms that day. Even so, it was very uncomfortable, sitting astride the narrow wooden structure. She had to hand it to Luke from the Garden Centre, he made a sturdy fence. With one hand, she managed to grasp the top of her little ladder and swing it over the fence, dropping it on the other side.

"For the love of -" Claudia swore roundly. "That was my foot, you know!"

Eve stifled a giggle and murmured, "Sorry. Can you put it somewhere safe?"

With more caution than dignity or grace, she got her foot on the step and lowered herself down. Most of the gardens that backed onto the field had a six foot border of thorns and undergrowth growing right up to their fence, but hers was the only garden with a clear spot, without many obstacles. She looked around her, trying to make out shapes in the gloom.

Her mother spoke right at her ear, causing her yet another mini heart attack.

"It's different at night, isn't it?" Niamh said gleefully. "You'd never think you were surrounded by houses, and a main road."

It was true. There was hardly a light in a window to break the night, and the place was eerily - unnaturally - quiet. But despite this, she felt quite at home, and perfectly safe.
"It's - it's nice, really. Calm."

"Come on," Dymphna instructed. "Let's get on with it."

What "it" was, Eve still had no idea. She tramped along behind the others, occasionally tripping over a rabbit hole, or an uneven patch of ground, or indeed, her own feet. The senior group waltzed across the ground as if it was brightly lit, and as smooth as ice.

"Here's as good as anywhere," Dymphna said, coming to a halt. They were now in the middle of the field, roughly speaking. Eve looked up at the night sky, the cold clear air making the stars dazzle overhead. The occasional tiny rustle in the grass beside her was the only sound, and the trees around the edges of the green were just a mass of shadows.

The five women stood still, soaking in the atmosphere.
"The energy of this place," Dymphna said solemnly, "Tune into it, Eve. Tell us what you feel."

For once, Eve didn't immediately say no, or that she couldn't. She didn't need to be told to feel the energy, it was as simple as breathing in or out. On the surface was the natural energy a place has from years of wild growth, wild things. Underneath though, there was a different energy. Energy that welcomed humans, wanted company, needed to be occupied.

For a moment, she wondered if the land wanted to be built on, to be filled with houses - and a feeling came, like a drizzle of cold water down her spine. Then she thought of the kids - Jenny, and her friends, the Marrinans, the primary school kids that Margaret taught - and her heart swelled, with the joy of the land.

"Oh, it's meant for the kids" the words were out before she could think. Her companions nodded at each other, and her mother patted her on the shoulder. "Good girl, that's what we needed to know."

"It's got a lot of natural energy, this place," Dymphna remarked. "We just weren't sure whether it was Brí or Bua."

Eve thought fast. Her mother had banged on and on about these things when she was younger, but it had been years since she had thought about them.

"Brí, the wild energy of a place. Bua, the energy a place gets from human usage." she parroted, unable to resist a smug glance at the older women. Claudia sniffed.

"Yes, well done. Good to see some of your mother's lessons stuck. Now, we need to get some rest. Early start in the morning, come on."

They started back towards the fence, Eve still buzzing from the experience. At last, it seemed she had found something she was good at, something the others needed her to do. Despite their reassurances, she had been feeling like a bit of a liability. Each of them had their own special areas of interest, and *"I'm not sure if I can do anything,"* wasn't one of them.

Secretly, she thought, "Maybe I can practice this, see if I can do it anywhere else." With the protest, her work, and Tom, and family and now the Christmas holidays coming up, she wouldn't have a lot of time for experimenting. Still, there was no rush - the new year would be quieter. She could go on a trip out to the mountains, or up to the Hill of Tara. If you couldn't feel something at Tara, there was no hope for you.

Lost in happy thoughts, she almost screamed when Claudia shot out a hand and caught her arm in a steel grip. In the dark, it was impossible to make out the expression on her face, but her body was as still as a statue. Eve couldn't hear any sound from either Niamh or Dymphna, either. Her heart thumping, she tried to freeze on the spot too.

A light flashed somewhere to the left of her, in the direction of her own garden fence. A thin line of illumination, bobbing and weaving - a torch, held by someone making their way over uneven ground. There was a slight disturbance in the air beside her, like a balloon popping silently - Dymphna was doing her own special trick, off to see what was happening.

"Ah!" A female voice, one that sounded familiar in a vague way, let out a quiet exclamation of disgust. "Bloody bat! God, I hate those things."

"Shut up!" A male voice pleaded. "Someone will hear."

"Oh, don't be such a wimp. Ugh, if I had a shovel I'd make short work of that thing. Where's it gone now? It went straight for my head, I swear."

"Dolores, it's just a bat, it can't hurt you. Please, keep your voice down."

"Oh, be quiet yourself. Keep looking, there has to be some sign of it. A large stone, with markings…"

"It's no use, there's only one clear patch along the whole fence. We haven't a hope of finding it, not in the dark."

Eve closed her eyes and concentrated on the male side of the whispered conversation. "Dolores" had to be McIntyre, the woman who had been bossing around the construction workers the previous week. Her accent, with its mix of Northern Ireland and something else, was very distinctive. She didn't recognize the man, but she was determined to memorize that voice. It was hard when someone was trying not to be heard, but she could pin point - under the rather affected, middle class drawl - a hint of something else. Flatter vowels, different rhythm. A Dublin accent, maybe Northside. Eve had always been good with sound - she could memorize a tune, even if her singing voice wasn't brilliant. And she was fairly sure, if she heard it again, she could recognize the mysterious companion that was traipsing around the dark with that awful McIntyre woman.

"You're right. We'll just have to wait until we can rip all this up - it won't be long now. Wait - what was that?"

The woman's voice sank to an urgent yelp, as a sound cut through the night, a low braying that was a cross between a fog horn and a constipated cow. Even Claudia's nerves of steel gave way, and she squeaked in fright. Eve heard her mother gasp, and Greta swore roundly, albeit very quietly.

"I have no idea - and I'm not staying here to find out!" the man snapped. The pair started moving rapidly, back towards where Eve and the others were standing. "They're going to run right into us," Eve thought frantically. An arm wrapped around her shoulder, and her mother whispered, "Don't move," in her ear. Claudia moved even closer, and Greta wrapped her arms around them to form a circle.

Claudia muttered under her breath, and Eve felt the strangest sensation. The solid ground beneath her feet melted away, the air seemed thinner, the dark even more intense. She felt, rather than saw, Dolores and her companion hasten past them, oblivious to their presence. As soon as they were a decent distance away, Claudia drew a deep breath and said, rather shakily, "That was close."

There was a faint "pop" and Dymphna emerged from the dark, adjusting her clothes and brushing herself down. "Mind you, we have as much right to be here as they do. We could have said we were out looking for Eve's cat or something."

"I don't have a cat," Eve pointed out.

"They don't know that."

"But they might start suspecting when they notice there's no sign of a cat."

"Well, the cat is lost, so there wouldn't be any sign of it, would there? Do think these things through, Eve."

She gave up. Arguing with the old ladies was like punching mist. In the end you were more likely to punch yourself in the face, than touch them.

"I'm exhausted," Claudia admitted, as they made their way over to the back of Eve's garden. "I think I'll head home, and get some sleep. I'll be back over first thing - see you on the picket line!"

Eve helped the ladies back over into her property. Dymphna was looking strained, and only Greta and Niamh seemed to have any energy left at all. She herself was ready for bed.

"I'll drop you two home," Niamh said to her friends. "Eve, pet, see you tomorrow."

Eve waved them off, climbed into bed and slept a deep and dreamless sleep.

Chapter 8

Early the following morning, Eve trudged her way from Bramble Lane to the main road, where the builders had set up their access entrance. The protest would take place right there, forcing the workers to cross the picket if they wanted to enter the green space – hence her braving the cold and dark at the unholy hour of six a.m.

Everyone will be in town doing their Christmas shopping, Eve thought pessimistically. I bet it'll just be a handful of us old fogeys, and that McIntyre woman sneering at us.

She had slept deeply after the excursion to the field with the others, but the feelings of elation and confidence had evaporated with the wintry morning sun. The construction workers had moved so quickly and there had been no time to organize a proper protest, she thought. In her old house, in a purpose built enclave on the outskirts of Dublin, with individual houses encased in high walls, and locked gates, it would have taken a year of residents committee meetings and full blown PR campaign to get anyone out for a protest. She smiled wryly at the thought of her old neighbours – Jacyntha with her helmet of perfect hair, Mona with her six inch nails and personal trainer who never seemed to actually do any training – out holding placards and chanting, "Save our Green."

Ah well, at least the old reliables would be there, she thought as she turned into Merrion Road and the entrance to the proposed building site came into view. Even in the dark, she could make out more than the five or six she had expected… there had to be at least twenty people there, she realized. In fact the closer she came, the more evident it was that despite the hour and the cold, a large crowd had gathered.

"Eve!" Claudia Warren called to her, her voice vibrant with triumph. "Over here!" The Brigadier held a clipboard in one hand - the perfect image of efficiency only slightly marred by the large unicorn topper on her pen.

"Well, it seems Bramble Lane isn't alone in despising this new development. Most of these people are from Merrion Road, and even a few from Abbeyville and beyond. Look – I have 43 names already. And most say they're staying for the morning but have someone coming to take their place this afternoon."

"It's amazing," Eve smiled. "You did a great job organizing."

"I can't take much credit, Eve. That young Jenny and her friends – and the primary school kids – all of them have taken the issue to the highest authorities. Their parents! One woman said her son badgered her into attending, and said he'd do the dishes for a week if she did."

"Well, whatever it takes! I'm just glad they're all here. Wait until McIntyre sees this!"

"And Finn Marrinan," Dymphna appeared at her elbow, her dark eyes flashing. "Don't forget our lovely neighbour."

"I'm sure once he realizes the strength of feeling about it all, he'll be more willing to compromise," Eve soothed her friend. "So, what's the plan?"

"Ah. Tom and some of the men have chained up the gate and

are building a kind of barricade behind it. A JCB would make short work of it, but you have to remember the optics, it's all about a good media story." Claudia winked at Eve. "Don't look so surprised, young woman. You don't get to be friends with Greta Goode for sixty years without picking up some tips. Speaking of whom, she and her Goode Hunters crew are liaising with the media as we speak."

"The media?" Eve felt a bit lightheaded. This was a lot more than she had bargained for.

"Yes, well done, your work really paid off. Every local newspaper is there and half the nationals, two radio stations have already mentioned the issue this morning – and Greta rounded up half a dozen of those beautiful, young things – whatyacallems, "Influencers"– they're all down taking selfies at the barricade. You mother is with them, she's taking a load of young politics students from UCD around the site, and she has the environmental protection crew eating out of her hand. There's a nice young lady up to her bum in brambles, looking for signs of a rare kind of field mouse."

"And," Dymphna interjected smugly, "I had a word with young Ronan Desmond, who had a word with his sergeants, who arranged for their team to police the event. Sergeant Jo Maguire, that would be."

As Josephine Maguire,a newly appointed sergeant, was Greta Goode's granddaughter, this was the equivalent of a match on home turf. Not that she wouldn't be fair, but she was unlikely to be overly persnickety about the smaller issues – like erecting barricades and chaining gates together.

Eve felt a surge of pride. She had once heard Dymphna, and by association, the other senior women, referred to as an "old Bat," and it had rankled. But here were the four old wans, fighting to save something that would benefit others and long outlast them. She had to swallow hard and blink a few times, before she could trust herself to say, "Well done, I'm dead impressed."

A couple of security guards were pleading with the protesters to get down off the barricade. One of them, the burly man with a goatee beard that Eve recognized from their first encounter with Dolores, was waving his arms furiously and practically jumping up and down in agitation. She bit back a smile, the unfortunate man looked so comical. His antics left Tom and his comrades unmoved, however. They just waved back cheerfully and continued to sit there.

The sky was still dark, and would be until half seven at this time of year. Cars passing them still had their headlights on, and the occasional pedestrians were muffled up, scarves around mouths and hoods or hats pulled well forward. It really was a bitterly cold morning. December in Ireland can be a toss-up between crisp and chilly, or wet and utterly miserable, Eve thought. Thankfully, it had turned out cold and dry. She glanced at the houses on the main Merrion Road. Many had already put up outdoor lights for the holidays, and quite a few were lit up, brightening the gloom of the morning. Around her was a very mixed bag of young mothers with buggys, students, retirees, men and women putting in an hour at the protest before work, and even a nun from the Convent of the Miraculous Mary. Two of the students were dressed in what looked like robes, and they were shyly banging bodhrán drums softly. A woman beside her touched the hedge of Brambles reverently and muttered a prayer, to what deity Eve had no idea. A lady in a colourful Dupatta smiled at her as she passed, offering a tray of Baklava pieces.

It seemed the importance of this little piece of green, wild land went beyond amenities and politics. She was looking around when she saw a pair of teenagers, with flaming red hair, standing close to the gate and peering over it. She recognized them as the pair she had met on her way home from art class, carrying armfuls of hay. When she waved at them, the girl frowned and then smiled, waving back. The boy nodded shyly. Eve racked her brains for the names Jenny had given her – Ashleigh and Sean.

The security team were now in a huddle, the man with the goatee at the centre. She supposed he was some kind of supervisor, and pitied him. The man was in for a rough day.

"Look!" Dymphna grabbed her arm and pointed to the edge of the crowd.

Another pair of young people stood there, one tall and broad-shouldered and the other petite. Boyd Marrinan and his sister Melly. They saw her, and she waved them over. After a moment's hesitation, they made their way across.

"Hi, Ms. Caulton." Boyd greeted her, his face serious. "This is a good turnout."

"Hi Boyd, Melly. Yes, it's better than we could have hoped." She paused, not sure what to say. It was awkward enough, with their father being public enemy number one at the moment. "You came to see what was happening, I suppose?"

Boyd flushed. "We're not here to spy, if that's what you think."

"Boyd!" Melly hushed him. "That's not what she meant, was it?"

"No, of course not. Apologies, Boyd, I phrased that badly."

"Oh. Sorry. I'm a bit on edge, I guess."

"I do understand," Eve said gently. "I've two kids, older than you pair now, but they're not so old that I don't remember. It's hard enough to fit in to a strange place without being caught in the middle of all this. But you shouldn't worry about it. Whatever happens, it's not your fault, and no one blames you. No one even blames your parents, for that matter. It's just...two sets of wants colliding. They want to develop this land and we want to preserve it and make it a communal asset. We'll work it out, eventually."

Boyd shook his head. "You *should* blame them. This isn't the first time this has happened. Why do you think we're here? We used to live in a town in Illinois, until Dad got wind of some land going and bought it. Then he built a factory on it, and ruined the whole place. No one would even speak to us, by the time it was all over. I had to leave the hockey team, Melly had to quit gymnastics." He looked on the verge of tears. "And now, he's doing it all over again."

"Oh, Boyd." Eve's heart went out to the boy. "Well, that's not going to happen here, I swear it. Jenny and Mikey, and that gang, they know who your dad is, don't they? Have they dropped you? No.Well, then!"

"They're cool," Boyd conceded. He glanced around. "There are some very cool people here. But I'm not going to let Dad wreck this place, the way he did Mountain Heights."

"*We're* not going to," Melly added stoutly. "Neither of us. That's why we're here."

"We're going to join the protest," Boyd said. "Let the newspapers report that! *Developers own kids are against him!* – I bet that'll go viral."

Eve started at him. "Boyd, that's a very big step to take. I know you feel strongly about it, but going against your parents so publicly – it's pretty hard to undo that. Maybe you should wait, for now. Tell him how you feel, and see what he says –"

"Ms. Caulton, ma'am, no offense, I can tell you mean well. But this is a free country, right? And this protest is open to everyone in the area who wants to save that field? Well, then. We're here and we're going to help."

Eve sighed. "I'm not stopping you from staying, or even helping. What I am saying is, don't court the media – not yet. Don't go looking to escalate things."

Boyd shrugged. "I'll think about it. Come on, Melly." He pulled his little sister away, pushing back through the throng until he reached the gate, where he took up a defiant stance. Eve shook her head. It would surely be very hurtful for the Marrinans to see their children on the other side of the issue to them – although, she had to admit to herself, her sympathies lay with the kids. What possessed Finn and Ellen to do the very same thing that had caused so much trouble in America?

"Probably, because it went so badly wrong there," Niamh said quietly. As a child, Eve had often been sure that her mother could read her mind and she was still half convinced.

"Sorry," Niamh continued, "Couldn't help overhearing. My guess is, Finn and Ellen's egos took a bruising back home. They were successful, in one sense, but lost everything that made that place home – friends, their kids' happiness, a sense of belonging. So, here they are, trying to prove to themselves that they can do it properly this time."

Eve was about to reply but a shout from the back of the crowd drowned her out. There was a scuffling movement, and the protesters parted slightly to reveal McIntyre, flanked by a group of large, muscular builders. She was dressed in jeans and a puffy jacket, with a bright red knitted hat on her head, pulled down low, instead of the yellow hard hat she usually wore.

"What the hell do you fools think you're doing?" the woman roared, her face contorted with rage. "Get out of the way before we run you over!"

The men behind her looked a little taken aback at her words, but glared at the crowd in a show of solidarity. Only the one Eve had noticed early, the one she thought of as the supervisor, looked askance at Dolores and murmured something. She responded impatiently and repeated, "Move or I'll move you with the JCBs!"

"We're going nowhere!" Dymphna strode forward, eyes blazing. "This is a legitimate protest, and if you touch any one of us, I'll have the Gardaí on you!"

As if conjured by those words, Sergeant Jo Maguire came into view, with her own entourage of large, sturdy, men and women.

"Good morning." She gave Eve the tiniest of winks, them being well acquainted since the unpleasantness earlier that year. She favoured Dolores with a stern look and said coldly, "Running people down is not a proper response to a peaceful protest, Ms. McIntyre."

"Peaceful? Look at my gate – look at that monstrosity!" The project manager pointed at the barricade of wooden pallets, old garden furniture, and bags of gravel from the Merrion Garden Centre – Luke had been most generous, Eve noted.

"Ah. Yes. Well, I can't answer for that," Jo said pleasantly. "That was there before we arrived. I did ask but no one could remember seeing anyone build it. Kids, I bet. You never know what mischief they'll be up to next."

"Cheek!" Jenny Chan called out.

"Hush now. Anyway, Ms. McIntyre, however it got there, it

is now in place. The gate is blocked by humans as well, and this is a protest which means you need to find some way around this that doesn't involve contravening the Road Traffic Act."

McIntyre took a step towards her, her hand extended and a finger wagging directly in the sergeant's face. Immediately two uniformed Gardaí stepped forward, and she paused. Jo glared at her, until the finger was lowered.

"This is a disgrace. A disgrace!"

"I'm sorry you feel that way, but we have a duty to prevent harm to persons, and to facilitate a safe and speedy resolution, with all due regards to public order," Sergeant Jo replied smoothly. "Are you the owner of this property?"

"What?" McIntyre seemed uncomfortable with the question. "That's neither here nor there. I'm the project manager and –"

"Get the owner down here," Jo advised sternly. "It's the owner we need. Now, who represents the protesters?"

Greta Goode took a step forward and Jo scowled at her. There was no way she was going to negotiate with her own grandmother, her expression said. Dymphna elbowed Greta and took her place.

"Mrs. Moriarty, Bramble Lane. And perhaps someone from Merrion Road?"

There was as murmur among the onlookers and by common consent, a woman with bright pink hair and colourful coat was pushed forward. She was one of the young women with a toddler in a buggy.

"I'm Chris Gannon, from Merrion."

Dymphna gave her a nod of approval. "Good woman. We're the spokespersons for the Save the Merrion Green Space Protest."

"Grand so," Jo said. "As ye were, people. Nothing to be done until the owner arrives. You give him a ring there, Ma'am, and we'll work from there."

McIntyre looked as if she'd like to box Jo's ears, but she pulled out her mobile and made the call. As she came to the end of what was evidently a terse conversation, her eye fell on Boyd and Melly and she pushed her way forward to confront them.

"Well, isn't this just lovely!" Eve could hear the anger in the woman's voice. McIntyre was delighted to find someone she could take her rage out on. She poked Boyd in the chest with one finger.

"If your father knew you were here, he'd hit the roof! Show a bit of loyalty, you jumped up little -"

"That's enough." Finn Marrinan strode through the crowd, his face set in grim lines. He glowered at McIntyre. "Go talk to Ellen, she's on the phone to our lawyers."

He waited until the disgruntled woman was out of earshot - but in ample range for Dymphna's acute hearing - before turning to his children.

"Melly, go to your mom. No - I don't want to hear it. Go stand with her, now." The girl looked at Finn, who nodded.

"It's not fair!" she said, but obeyed her father.

Finn shook his head sadly. "For god's sake, Boyd. Bad enough you get yourself mixed up in all this, but taking your sister along…what were you thinking? No, don't answer that. You thought it would hurt your mother and me, and I guess you were right. You must have known this protest was going to happen, but you didn't care enough about your own family to give us a heads-up. I give up. You really have let us down, and worse, you've let yourself down."

"Sure. Blame me." Boyd sneered, his eyes blazing. "You never take any responsibility, do you? You went back into partnership with that awful woman, after everything she did! You're the one ruining this place, upsetting all these people but sure, yeah, it's all my fault. Well, fine. Now you know how I feel, and Melly too. We're on their side, not yours. And we'll do anything we can to make sure you don't tear up this field."

Finn tried to catch his arm as Boyd pushed past him, but the boy shook him off. "Leave me alone, Dad. You go bully those old women…you're done telling me what to do!"

Eve had watched the exchange closely, the conversation loud enough to reach her and a lot of others standing around. Her heart went out to the younger Marrinan, but his dad's face was such a picture of misery, she couldn't help feel sorry for him too. She watched Boyd wind his way through the protesters and Gardaí towards his mother, who was standing with the locked-out builders. He put his arm around Melly and hugged her, whispering something in her ear.

Dolores McIntyre stepped forward and in a voice that could be heard even over the noise of the crowd, said "I hope your dad put some manners on you, you ignorant pup!"

Boyd looked her up and down, and said coldly, "You're a snake, McIntyre, and my parents should never have taken up with you. You're leeching off them, you're ruining everything -again. I know all about you and your dealings. You're as crooked as a corkscrew but nowhere near as useful."

The project manager stepped forward, her arm raised as if to slap him. Ellen Marrinan jumped between them, and caught the other woman by the shoulder.

"Stop that! How dare you hit him?"

"He's a sneaky little rat, your son!" Dolores snapped. "Spoiled brat…he's behind all this. How else would they get into the site and cause all this havoc?"

"We let ourselves in," Tom called, brandishing a pair of bolt cutters (probably also donated by the Merrion Garden Centre, Eve thought.)

"I don't care," Ellen said quietly. "It's not your place to speak to him like that."

Dolores snorted. "That's rich. I've just as much invested in this project as you do. Get your brat under control!"

Eve looked at the others. This was news. She had assumed Dolores McIntyre was an employee, a hired gun. Boyd had spoken as if she was more than that and now she was talking as if she was a partner, not an employee. But she had told Sergeant Maguire that Finn owned the land.

"I told you," Ellen said, squaring up to McIntyre, "Leave him alone."

"I can talk for myself," Boyd interjected. "I don't care what she says about me."

Dolores narrowed her eyes. "You should care, little man. You'll regret crossing me. I'll make you regret it."

"Yeah? Try it - I'll finish you!"

Unfortunately, Boyd raised his voice just as the noise of the crowd lulled; the words "I'll finish you" rang out clearly, just in time for Detective Sergeant Ronan Desmond and his partner Detective Garda Mick Cullen to hear.

Chapter 9

"Well, that was some day!" Greta Goode sank into Eve's largest armchair and stretched. "I thought that Dolores woman would explode, when Boyd told her she was a crook!"

"What a wagon!" Claudia sniffed. "I understand Finn and Ellen being annoyed at Boyd, but Dolores McIntyre had no right to speak to him like that."

"Ronan gave her short shrift," Tom grinned, as he passed out mugs of hot tea and coffee. The afternoon had turned very cold, and revolutionary fervour could only do so much against the freezing damp of a Dublin December.

"He did. It was a delight to watch."

Detective Desmond and his partner had imposed order on what threatened to turn into a public brawl between Ellen and Dolores. The Gardaí were slightly bewildered when they realized both women were ostensibly on the same side, but soon grasped that McIntyre was the instigator. The irate project manager - or indeed, partner – hadn't helped her case by calling Detective Cullen a "lump of lard," and "a lazy git."

Ronan Desmond had stepped back, and let the full wrath of the older Garda descend on the woman. It was a far quieter Dolores McIntyre who retreated from the field of battle, to the delight of the protesters, a sizable crowd of morning commuters and passers-by, and even some of her own work crew. The builders tried to be discreet but couldn't hide their smiles.

After that, Finn and Ellen also disappeared. The protesters stood their ground, with reinforcements arriving in the afternoon.

"We'll have people here all night," Jenny had assured them. "Even my dad volunteered to take a shift. They'll be hoping we go home and they'll sneak in and dismantle the barricade, but they've another think coming. No one is getting in or out of that field tonight but us."

Eve was bone weary and not just from the day's activities. It was the start of December, and she had expected to be occupied with shopping for presents, and visiting friends – not fighting with builders. Why did nothing ever go according to plan? Mairead had already been on to her twice that day, once when she heard about the protest and then again to say she could see her mother on the RTE lunchtime news.

"For god's sake, Mam! After everything that just happened, would you not take it easy for a while? I even had Dad texting me, asking why were you dressed like a hippie waving a placard. He says it doesn't reflect well on him, lots of people still think of you as his wife."

"Well, I'm not!" Eve had snapped, stung to tears by the injustice. "Your father decided that I wasn't good enough to have as a wife any more, or have you forgotten? And I won't apologize for standing up for what's right."

Mairead had apologized immediately, but Eve couldn't shake off a miserable feeling over it all. She hated confrontation with anyone, least of all her own kids. Liam had also texted, but in typical Liam style it had just read, "*Good on you, Mam! Up the Revolution."* She could shave her head and turn Kimberly Cottage into a commune and Liam would just ask if she was happy.

Mairead worried, god help her.

Tom put his arm around her shoulders. "You all right, love?"

Eve smiled at him. "Yeah. Just a bit tired. Not exactly what I had hoped to be doing this week."

"I know. I wanted to take you into town and see the lights. There's a huge tree at Stephen's Green, all lit up and the whole of Grafton street, and all the little streets – they look magical."

"Maybe we'll get in on the weekend," Eve said. "Til then, we can man the barricades."

She was relieved when everyone opted to go home, rather than sit around chatting. Even the indomitable Dymphna looked exhausted. Eve waved them off, promised to call for Tom early the next morning, and settled down to an evening of TV and a microwaved meal.

Despite her low mood, turning on the Christmas tree lights and reading a few chapters of her new book - a paperback, called "Mistletoe and Murders" from the local library, combining three dastardly murders with a lovely Christmas themed sub plot - cheered her up. She made a cuppa and turned on the evening news, laughing at the sight of Dymphna and Greta shaking their fists and shouting *"Save the Green"* like elderly revolutionaries. Feeling much more cheerful, she decided to watch TV for a while and then crawl to bed.

She was dozing in front of the latest episode of "Abandoned" – fourteen completely unprepared eejits dropped in the wilderness of West Clare, with only a spork and a penknife, to survive for a fortnight – when an eerie sound, the sound of a cow singing while strangling a cat, jerked her awake.

"What the giddy…" She sprang to her feet, heart pounding. That was the second time she had heard that sound, the last time being in the field behind her house late last night. The sound that had sent McIntyre and her friend scurrying.

"We never did talk about that," she realized. "What on earth were they up to out there?" But there was no time to consider it now. The noise had faded away, leaving an eerie silence in its wake.

She stood listening, her ears straining but there were only the normal evening sounds of a suburb. There was little light and even her own back garden was a shadowy mirage of shapes and shadows. She was about to give up when a very different, but distinct sound reached her ears.

The sound of someone, or something, systematically pounding against her fence.

Without pausing to think, she grabbed her keys and unlocked the back door, stepping out into the night. The sound was deafening, now it was unfiltered by double glazing. Instinctively she glanced at Dymphna's house, expecting the old lady to be leaning out her bedroom window by now, but it was in darkness. There was no sign of life at the back of any of the other cottages, either.

"How could anyone sleep through that racket!" Eve armed herself with a yard brush and crept forward towards the noise. To her horror, several boards cracked and splintered as she watched - buckling inwards under some huge, unseen force.

Eve ran the rest of the way down the garden path, brandishing the heavy yard brush like the sword of an avenging angel.

"*Gaaaaaaaaaah!*" she screamed, possibly the least eloquent war cry in the history of Ireland, but it did the trick in so far as the noise stopped, and the fence ceased to crumble.

Panting, she clambered onto a patio chair, and peered over the now misshapen boards, into the dark empty space beyond. There was nothing, not a sign of life, and no sign of whoever - or whatever - had destroyed her garden boundary for the second time. Eve blinked, trying to force her eyes to see into the night, until she gave it up as a bad job and went back into the house to retrieve her mobile phone.

"What did we do without these yokes?" she muttered, resuming her perch. "Now, let's see…where's my torch function?"

The phone torch sent out a surprisingly bright beam, illuminating only a small patch at a time, but doing that well. She moved it steadily across the ground, noting the shrubs and brambles that grew up to the fence seemed undamaged, but the ground directly behind her wooden fence, the one clear patch that was free of thorns and dense undergrowth, had some marks and cuts. There was no sign of whatever had stood there, however.

Eve closed her eyes and tried to see in a different way.

There was the land, silent and waiting, almost ominous in its quietness…there were the trees, so steady and slow, their bare limbs reaching to the cold night sky…there were the small creatures, little furry things that lived in the dark and trembled. She could feel them all, and something else, something that was big and strange and lurked just out of reach. It didn't belong there, but the land was filled with love towards it - there was something she didn't understand going on, but it wasn't bad. It wasn't why the creatures were afraid and the land subdued.

And then she felt it - the other thing that shouldn't be there, but this *was* bad. This was awful.

Her hands trembling she shone the torch light on a mis-shapen, lumpy patch of ground - no, she saw now, *not* ground. Not ground, not a pile of rags, not a bag of rubbish thrown there. A person, lying prone on the ground, with a distinctive red knitted hat and even in the poor light, even without climbing over to check, Eve knew the person was dead.

Dolores McIntyre was dead.

Chapter 10

Detective Desmond was once again in her living room, taking details from her regarding a dead person. Only a few months after the last one!

It was a nightmare. Eve choked back a sob and Tom appeared by her side, bearing tea and biscuits. Ronan sat opposite her, his face serious but kind. Dymphna was in the kitchen, making tea for the legion of Gardaí working their way through the field in the early hours of the morning, and the forensic teams. Dr Lorraine O'Toole, the state pathologist, had already spoken to her over the battered fence and put in a request for strong coffee, with several sugar lumps. Somehow, when she had examined Eve's living room a few months ago, when the last murder occurred on Bramble Lane, Dr O'Toole had become bosom buddies with Dymphna, and indeed seemed to be on excellent terms with all the old women. All of whom had, of course, descended on the place, the moment Dymphna had found time to text them.

There was something comforting in their presence, Eve had to admit. They filled up spaces that no one else would think about - tea for the poor sods out in the bitter cold, breaking the news to neighbours but tactfully keeping them at bay, soothing those who were upset and giving bracing advice to those inclined to dramatics.

She dragged her attention back to Ronan.

"I'm sorry, what did you say?"

"It's okay, Eve. You've had a shock. I was just asking how you came to be in your back garden at that hour."

"The fence," Eve said, surprised he even had to ask. "I heard the most almighty battering out the back, and ran out. Something was bashing away at the new fence, it's splintered and bent again. I climbed up on a garden chair to look over and –" she shuddered, "Saw that poor woman."

Everyone was silent now, even Dymphna had abandoned her post in the kitchen to stand in the doorway and listen. Eve described how she used her phone torch, "But I couldn't see anything strange, nothing that would explain the fence. Then I – um, I thought I'd give it one last sweep with the torch – and saw the body."

Ronan nodded sympathetically. "You acted very swiftly, Eve, thanks to you the scene is being preserved and forensics have a fighting chance. If she'd lain there til morning, with the rain forecast, we would be lucky to get anything."

He stood up, anxious to get out to the action himself. Glancing at his watch he added, "I'll talk to you again in the morning, but for now, get some rest. Someone should stay with her," he added to the room at large.

"I will," both Dymphna and Niamh chorused. The two women looked at each other and chuckled.

"Sure, both of us will. Eve can sit up or go lie down as she pleases. We'll mind her."

"Don't be daft, Mam!" Eve appealed to Ronan. "It's the middle of the night, they can't be sitting up in my armchairs til morning." She didn't add "at their age," but it hung on the air between them.

"And they won't have to," Tom said firmly. "Ladies, both of you need sleep. Niamh, why not stay over with Dymphna for the rest of the night, you'll be nearby if needed, and I'll mind Eve."

Niamh opened her mouth to protest but a sharp elbow in the ribs from Dymphna silenced her.

"That's the best solution," Dymphna said, a dirty big grin across her face. "Well now, Eve, isn't it nice to have a big strong man around the house? Maybe you wouldn't go around finding dead bodies all the time, if Tom was here to keep an eye on you."

Eve couldn't find the words to express her outrage, especially considering Dymphna Moriarty's views on the general use-lessness of the male species. Dymphna winked at her, gathered up a reluctant Niamh and all her belongings and ushered her out the door. Ronan looked at Eve and a red-faced Tom sympathetically.

"They're on at me and Margaret too," he sighed. "Like, I'm definitely going to ask her to move in, but – well, I know it sounds silly but I want to ask her something else first."

Before Eve or Tom could react, the detective blushed, smiled bashfully and made his escape.

"Did he just tell us he's going to propose to Margaret Furey?" Tom asked.

"I think he did." Eve grinned, a sudden realization hitting her. "He wanted to cheer me up, so he let us in on the secret."

"Ah. He's a nice lad, isn't he?"

"A very nice young man. Well, at least that's some good news. Oh, Tom!" She couldn't stop her lip from quivering. "Christmas is ruined," Eve burst into tears, the sadness welling up in her over the past week bursting out.

Tom put his arms around her and let her weep, until she managed to sniff, and mumble, "Sorry! It all just got to me."

"I know, Love. But listen to me. This is an awful thing, no doubt about it. And we'll have reporters and media and all that nonsense again. Two murders in such a short time, in a quiet suburb – it's bizarre. But we're still going to have a nice Christmas. We're going to get into town and see the lights, go shopping, buy each other silly presents that no one else will understand and even go see a show. The Gaiety Panto, if I can get tickets."

"Sure, you won't get tickets for that -they're sold out in July," Eve said. "But I appreciate the sentiment."

"We'll do *something* nice. And your kids will come for the holidays, and my brother and sister-in-law are dying to meet you. And there'll be a party for all our friends on Bramble Lane – I'll even invite the Marrinans, cheer them up too. After all, they knew that woman quite well. Even if they didn't get on."

Eve suddenly remembered the altercation between Boyd and Dolores, at the protest.

"Oh, it's a good job this happened in the middle of the night, Tom. Imagine if people thought Boyd had carried out his threat."

"Ah, no one will. He only said that in response to her threats."

"But most people only heard what he said, they didn't hear what led up to it."

"Well, he'll be asleep in his bed at the time, you'll find. So don't worry about it."

Eve gave herself a stern mental shake. "I'm letting my imagination run away with me."

"You're exhausted. Everything seems awful right now. Go up to bed, pet, I'll clear up this lot."

Eve climbed the stairs wearily, feeling a lot better knowing Tom was in the house. *Maybe*, she thought, as sleep finally overtook her poor, overwrought brain, *maybe it wouldn't be a bad thing to have Tom around the place, permanently.* Of course, it was far too soon – but at their age, what was too soon? Life, she thought, was very short when you looked at it.

It was late morning when she woke, and even then Eve would have slept longer if the noise of banging hadn't woken her. An irate, but by now familiar voice, was bellowing outside her house.

"Finn, what the hell are you doing?" Tom's normally calm voice sounded outraged. Like a stern schoolmaster, Eve couldn't help laughing to herself.

"Where is she? I know she's in there!"

"Finn, please!" Ellen's voice – sounding close to tears.

"I need to talk to her, Tom." All of a sudden, Finn sounded pleading, all the belligerence drained away.

Eve hopped out of bed, pulled her fleece dressing gown around her and called down the stairs, "Come in, for goodness sake. I'm coming down."

She found the Marrinans and Tom in her living room, Tom standing with his arms crossed, still looking stern and cross, in full warrior mode. Finn and Ellen stood by her fireplace, side by side but not touching, both with strained, miserable faces.

"What on earth is going on?" Eve sat down on an armchair. "In case you haven't realized, I've had a rotten night. This is the last thing I needed."

"You've had a rotten night? That's rich –" Finn started, but

Ellen cut across him,

"Eve, please. You have to tell them you were mistaken. It couldn't have been Boyd you saw, it couldn't have been."

"Boyd? But I didn't see Boyd. Where am I meant to have seen Boyd?"

The couple exchanged a glance.

"At the murder scene," Finn said. "We were told an eye-witness saw Boyd leaving the scene. And you were the only eyewitness so –"

"No." Eve shook her head. "Yes, I saw the body but only after the fact. I saw no one else, and certainly not Boyd. It must have been someone else, I'm afraid."

"At two in the morning?" Finn sounded incredulous.

Eve thought for a moment. "The protesters, Finn. We organized a skeleton crew to man the barricade in shifts through the night. They must have seen – well, someone must have thought they saw your son."

"Oh God…" Ellen covered her face with her hands. "I'm so sorry. Please forgive us for bursting in like this."

"Don't be daft." Eve winced, realizing she sounded just like her mother, bracing and no nonsense. "I mean, it's totally understandable. Tom, put the kettle on. Sit down, the pair of ye, and tell me what's happened."

Finn's shoulders slumped, all the fight gone from the man.

"What's happened? Eve…they've arrested Boyd on suspicion of murder."

Chapter 11

"Detective Desmond and his partner, Cullen - they came to tell us the news. With that young sergeant." Ellen sobbed.

"Sergeant Maguire." Eve supplied the name.

"Yes, that's her. They asked us about Dolores, how we knew her, how long she'd worked for us. Then one of them brought up that stupid argument yesterday – between Boyd and Dolores."

"I remember. But that was just talk."

"Of course it was," Finn interrupted his wife's recital. "Boyd wouldn't hurt anyone."

"*We* know that," Ellen snapped, "But the cops think it was a threat. Anyway, they asked to speak to Boyd, and I went to wake him up – but he wasn't there. I woke Melly and she admitted that Boyd snuck out last night. He was still angry with us and she thinks he was going to..to the protest."

Eve noted the woman's hesitation and made a mental note – Ellen wasn't saying quite everything. Perhaps to spare Finn's feelings or perhaps because Melly admitted Boyd had plans other than to help at the barricade. But for now, she let her neighbour continue.

"Anyway, the moment they realized he wasn't in the house all hell broke loose. They insisted on leaving the sergeant there to wait for him. She asked us to ring around his friends but who? We're only here a few weeks yet – he doesn't really know anyone."

"Jenny Chan and her friends," Eve exclaimed. "They've all become close over the last while. I have her number, I'll ring her."

"It's too late now. Boyd waltzed in at eight o'clock, bold as brass and refused to tell anyone where he was or what he'd been up to. Just looked pleased with himself." Ellen blinked back tears. "Then the cop told him about Dolores McIntyre. He went white, and started shaking. I swear to God, he had no idea. Boyd is a terrible liar, he always was. Even as a toddler I knew when he was fibbing. He just isn't that good of an actor – it was obvious he didn't know she was dead."

"Of course," Eve said soothingly. "Ellen, no one in this room believes Boyd would kill her. But how did he end up being arrested?"

Finn took up the story. "The detectives came back, once Maguire told them Boyd had returned. They questioned him, but he refused point blank to tell them anything. Just kept saying, he couldn't tell. Over and over. Like, he was really sorry but it was impossible. Then they said an eyewitness had placed him at the scene, a positive identification. So – in the absence of an alibi or any explanation about why he was there, they arrested him."

Eve had to admit, the Gardaí had little choice, but that was cold comfort to the boy's parents.

"Okay. Well, the first thing we need to do is find out who this eyewitness is and what exactly they saw. And of course, you need to get your solicitor down to the station. In fact, one of you should be there right now."

"I was going," Ellen said, "But Finn got it into his head it had to be you, and when he set off around here…"

"You came to stop him making things worse." Eve grinned at her. "It's all right, Finn, if it was one of mine I'd do the same thing. Maybe not quite as loudly – you scared the living daylights out of me! – but yeah, we'd all do anything for our kids."

Finn met her eyes, and nodded. "I am sorry, though."

"Accepted. Right, get going - both of you, off to the station and be with your son. Who's your solicitor?"

"We – I don't really know. We have a law firm for commercial stuff. Would they take this on?"

Eve thought for a moment. "You need Ms. Warren. You've met Mrs. Claudia Warren, the Brigadier in the Irish Women's Association? – her daughter is a criminal lawyer and absolutely excellent. She saved my bacon, I can tell you – long story, I'll explain another time. I'll ring her and see what she can do. But don't let them interview Boyd without a lawyer. Talk to Ronan, tell him Jennie Warren will be coming."

Fingers crossed, Eve thought privately, but if anyone could help Boyd it would be Claudia's daughter.

"Thanks." Ellen turned to her husband. "It'll be okay, Finn. We know Boyd is innocent."

Finn managed a smile, hugging her fiercely. "Go on. I'll meet you there. I'll get someone to stay with Melly."

"Bring her next door, my mam and Dymphna will mind her. " Eve said. "Tom, if I give you Jenny Chan's number will you get in touch with her, see if any of her lot met Boyd last night?"

"Will do. What are you going to do?"

"I'm going to find our eyewitness, and see what we can piece together about last night." Eve paused, and then gave in to the inevitable. "And I'll get Claudia and Greta too. Might as well get the whole gang together."

Finn looked at her curiously. "The gang?"

"Ah. This isn't our first rodeo, as you might say. My mother and her friends might look like your typical auld wans, but they have a lifetime of nosiness and meddling behind them. They're better than any team of detectives when they get going. Trust me, if anyone can find out what Boyd was up to last night – it's them."

Finn sighed. "I'll take all the help I can get, from any source. To be honest, I feel bad now. I have to admit I thought Mrs. Moriarty was a right old bat."

Eve laughed, the first genuine merry laugh in what felt like a long time.

"Oh, Finn, she is. You have no idea. But she's our old bat. They all are. You're in good hands, believe me."

Chapter 12

The protest was still in place, although the barrier had been removed to allow the Gardaí access to the crime scene. Thanks in part to Eve's hard work in getting the media to cover the protest, there had been media there on and off since the previous morning. Now, they were out in full force - television, print and online media. The crowd was standing at a respectful distance, their placards placed against the fence. At a bit of a loose end, the locals were milling around talking to each other, listening avidly to any snippet of news.

The Marrinans' security team were also standing around. The presence of the Gardaí made them rather redundant for the moment, but they held themselves apart from the protesters. Only one of them, the man with the goatee she recognized from the previous day, chatted to groups of locals. He was nodding along sympathetically to something a short, blonde woman was saying. Eve approached and joined the circle of people around her.

"I saw him, clear as day!" the woman said stubbornly. "Him and two other young wans, running across the field"

"It was pitch dark," a man chided her. "You couldn't have seen him clearly."

"Well, then, that's all you know! A car went by and they were caught in the headlights. I recognized him immediately – sure, wasn't he here earlier causing a fuss? He's the son of that Finn, the Yank who bought the land."

"Even so, it was the middle of the night. I couldn't swear to recognizing someone I barely knew, in a few seconds, in the dark."

"Are you not listening? I told you, I saw him clearly and I have a very good memory for faces…"

After fifteen minutes of listening to this back and forth, Eve gave up with a sigh. This was going nowhere. The woman, who had introduced herself as Joan Farrell from Merrion Road, had been perfectly happy to answer questions put by her neighbours – eager, in fact. She was clearly relishing her time in the spotlight and with every attempt to cast doubt on her identification of Boyd, she became ever more convinced that she had seen him. Eve decided to leave her to her audience and see what else people had to say.

Public opinion at the protest site was divided. Some felt Joan was stretching the truth, and were adamant that they had seen nothing- no sign of Dolores McIntyre or Boyd entering the green space. Some few were sure that Boyd must had done it, simply because he was the son of the developer. Why he would have wanted to remove the project manager, they weren't sure but he was guilty by association. One, they said, he'd been seen arguing with McIntyre and obviously hated her and the proposed development, and two, he was obviously removing her on the orders of his parents, to make sure the development went through!

They seemed untroubled by the contradiction.

Most however, were just saddened by the whole event and sympathetic towards the Marrinans.

"I've a boy his age," one woman said, "It's every parents nightmare, them getting into trouble like that. Whether he did it or not, it's awful for the family."

She had caught the last of the night shift, before they made their way home to a warm breakfast and a nap. Joan Farrell had been on duty since two in the morning and would have left hours before if it wasn't for her role as star witness. She had told the story to each wave of reinforcements, since her conversation with the police.

"It was half past two," she repeated, "and I saw them, like I can see you now!"

Before she left, Eve decided to try a different tack with Joan. She rejoined the group around her, and asked, "So, what did the other pair look like?"

"The ones with him? Eh, one was quite short, couldn't really see much of them – hoodie up, head down. But the other one, that was a girl. Tall, slim. Long hair, too, and now I think of it, her hair was red."

"Could the other one, the shorter one, have been a boy?" Eve tried not to sound too excited.

"Oh. Well, yes, to be honest, I sort of assumed it was."

"Great, thank you!"

Eve hurried away, needing to think. A tall, slim girl with long red hair and a shorter boy – the two teenagers she had bumped into in the dark, on her way home from classes. Jenny Chan had told her their names – what on earth were they, now? She racked her brains and suddenly recalled, Ashleigh and Sean.

"And she lives on Merrion Road!" Eve thought, then wondered, would Joan not have recognized the girl as a neighbour? Wait a minute, she thought, all Ashleigh had said that night was that they lived in a house that bordered the field. She may not have meant the main road.

She hastened out onto the main road and walked along it, noting the houses that backed onto the field. Merrion bordered it on two sides – up along the right hand side, and across the back opposite to Bramble Lane. But on the other side, there were a row of houses backing onto the field, another small group of homes rather like her own street.. Eve walked up to the turn, and paused, reading the sign. "Pine Tree Road," she read out loud, and smiled.

"I bet this is where they live, not on the main road. Joan probably wouldn't recognize a kid that isn't an immediate neighbour."

Dublin used to be the kind of place where you knew everyone in a two mile radius of your house, but time and the inexorable march of progress meant that people were often too busy or too isolated to know much about their neighbours. The lockdown during the pandemic had changed that a little – people realized the value of local community again – but still, with most people out of the house before eight a.m. and not home again before seven in the evening, there was a limit to how well you could know the area. Which made the turnout for the protest even more impressive, when you thought about it.

"Excuse me!" A woman with a toddler and a laden buggy full of shopping tapped Eve on the shoulder.

"Oh Excuse me! I didn't mean to block the path." Eve jumped aside to let her pass.

"No problem," the young woman smiled, "Are you looking for somewhere?"

"Actually, someone. I don't suppose you know a young girl,

tall with red hair, her name is Ashleigh –"

"Oh sure, yeah. She's in number eleven. Lovely girl, always very kind to my Ciarán – isn't she, love?"

The toddler turned a smiling face to his mammy and remarked solemnly, "Love Ash."

"Yes, you do! You love Ash, don't you. He really does," she turned back to Eve, "Ash and her brother often take him out for walks, and let him play in their garden – they have a swing set, mad yoke, their dad built for them. Before he died, you know. Awful nice family. Her mother is out working all hours, she's a great woman. But it does leave the poor kids on their own a lot."

Eve nodded, afraid to say anything that might stymie the woman's flow of interesting facts.

"I'd say the kids are at school by now. But they're usually home about half three, if you want to catch them."

"Oh thanks, I will do that. It's – it's about art classes," Eve felt she should offer some explanation.

The mother grinned broadly. "Oh wow. Are you a painter? I'd love to be able to paint. Not that I've any time for classes, not with this man swinging out of me, eh Ciarán?"

"Like paint." Ciarán informed Eve. "Like red, and yellow. And purple."

"Me too. They're some of my favourite colours. Well, thank you very much – I'm Eve, by the way. Eve Caulton.I live on Bramble Lane."

"Mags. Mags Phelan. Hey. If you hear of any mammy and baby art classes, let me know! I'm number fifteen."

"I will," Eve promised. In fact, she thought, maybe I should suggest that to the committee. Toddlers could paint little projects while parents had a chance to learn some techniques…

she filed it away for a less hectic moment. For now, it was time to get home and rally the troops.

As it turned out she didn't have much rallying to do – the troops had turned up of their own volition, needing absolutely no encouragement to interfere in the new investigation. In fact, if Eve was feeling uncharitable, she would have said that they were rather too happy to have an excuse to play detective again. Claudia had actually postponed a meeting of the Brigade's Fundraising committee, an event unprecedented in the history of her reign as Brigadier General, except for the unfortunate incident with the gas cooker and a birthday candle back in two thousand and seven. Greta was setting up a laptop to take notes for her podcast, and Dymphna had set Eve's table with buns, tea pot, her good china cups and five A4 writing pads.

"We'll need to take notes. I know, we all have phones, but for something like this I prefer pen and paper," her neighbour said. "Your mother has gone to the shops for some milk, and some decent biscuits. You've nothing in the house."

"Actually," Eve said smugly, "I've a stash of nice ones in the –" She stopped, as Dymphna shook her head.

"You *had* a stash. Greta found it in the first ten minutes, and with the Gardaí still combing the field, they didn't last long at all. Dear God, that young Garda they left on watch out there can put away a Swiss roll, all by himself."

Eve retreated to her sitting room, to find Tom and a rather sheepish Ronan Dempsey sitting there. Her Christmas tree was unlit, but someone had fixed a thick garland of holly and tinsel along the mantle piece. Tom pointed at it, and asked, "Do you mind? I was making one for myself and thought, that's what Kimberly cottage needs. No point in having a nice mantelpiece and not decorating it at this time of year!"

"It's lovely." And she had to admit, it definitely restored a little cheer to the place. They might be dealing with a death – again – but they didn't have to let it spoil everything.

She gave Ronan a sympathetic glance. "They roped you in, I see."

"Well, after last time – it seemed churlish to refuse their help. No one knows this area like those old women. And they seem to have a knack for finding things out."

A rap on the door announced Niamh's return, laden with bags of goodies.

"One thing I love about the holidays," she said, thrusting them at Eve, "All the bargains. Two for one on tubs of Roses chocolates. And half price on the Cadbury's."

"Mam! I'll never get through all of this."

"Have you met Greta?" Niamh muttered darkly. "I didn't even get a sniff of a choccie biscuit, she had the lot hoovered. And what she didn't eat, the cops savaged. Anyway, they won't go to waste. Sure, won't Liam and Mairead be here in a few weeks? Liam has a sweet tooth, he'll make short work of anything left over."

"Stop blathering," Dymphna ushered them all into the small kitchen. It was a crowd for such a limited space - Tom opted to stand, while Ronan perched on a rickety stool and the women arranged themselves around the table. Niamh stuck a mini chocolate roll into her mouth defiantly but took her place.

"Well, now. We have quite the problem on our hands." Dymphna waved her hand in the air, in the vague direction of the field. "Obviously, that woman was a plague and a pill, but no one deserves to be murdered. We find ourselves in a strange position, ladies – and you pair." She begrudgingly included Tom and Ronan. "We are naturally opposed to Finn and Ellen and their development. But Boyd, that's another matter."

"Boyd is a nice young fella," Greta agreed. "And if he did knock that wagon over the head, I bet he had good reason."

"Greta!" Niamh shook her head. "For goodness sake – murder is murder. It's never justified."

"Hah! That's what you say. Personally, I've investigated cases on my podcast where in my opinion, the murderer did everyone a favour."

"Greta!"

"Never mind her. Back to business, if you please. Now, we know that Boyd didn't do it – Oh, be quiet, Ronan Desmond. I've seen enough in my time to know what people are capable of, and Boyd is not capable of hurting a woman and leaving her in a field."

"Ronan is a garda," Eve reminded her. "He has to keep an open mind, and deal in facts. And the fact is Joan saw him, and two others, in that field around the time of the murder."

"Who's Joan?" Niamh hissed at Greta.

"Joan Farrell, the eyewitness."

Ronan groaned. "How did you find her?"

"Sure, she's down at the site telling anyone who'll listen."

"Oh for – I'll get Jo to have a word with her." He whipped out his mobile phone and started texting furiously. Greta smiled smugly, as she did every time her granddaughter was mentioned.

"Sergeant Jo Maguire," she looked around the table, grinning. "She's his right hand man, so she is."

"Woman," Claudia corrected her sternly. "Right hand woman. She is a marvel, though. She made short work of Dolores, when she was throwing her weight around."

"Dolores…we know very little about her, don't we?" Niamh reached for a chocolate digestive. "I mean, I thought she was just an employee of Finn's but then Boyd said she was a partner. And what about the other night?"

Dymphna gave her a warning look and a tiny shake of the head.

"The other night?" Tom asked.

"The night before last, she was out in the…oh. Um. I mean, she was hanging around."

Tom frowned. "When was this? And hanging around where?"

Dymphna rolled her eyes. "Look, the night before last, we were out in the field. Just…getting the lay of the land."

Ronan sat up, looking for all the world like an inquisitive hound.

"Were you, now? And did you see anything interesting?"

Eve interjected, "We were just looking to see if there was… any other entrance, other than the main gate. So they couldn't surprise us in the morning."

Ronan looked doubtful, but didn't press her. Niamh crammed another biscuit into her mouth and tried to avoid Dymphna's exasperated stare.

"While we were…looking around, we saw Dolores and a man – a stranger, not anyone we know – looking around. They seemed to be searching for something. Talked about needing to look in daylight and maybe dig up the ground."

Ronan looked disappointed. "Ah. Probably looking for old gas lines, or electricity cables. Pity, I thought we might have something there."

Eve hesitated. She didn't think that the pair were looking for anything as mundane as old utility pipes but If Ronan was happy with that interpretation, maybe they should let it be. It was hard enough to explain why the women had been out there at that hour, without trying to convey the feeling she had about that conversation.

"Can you describe the man she was with?" Ronan asked.

"Not really. He was about her height, I think, so not very tall. But he was well muffled up."

"Pity. Still, we'll look into it."

"Moving on, then. Who was Dolores, and what is her exact position in Finn's outfit?" Dymphna waited, then added impatiently, "Write it down, ladies!"

There was an obedient scratching of pens on paper. Greta tapped her pen against the table.

"I'll take her background, Dymphna. My followers will ferret out everything there is to know about her."

"Excellent. Number two - what was Boyd doing wandering around there in the middle of the night?"

"I'm already on that," Eve said. "I've an idea who the other pair were, that Joan saw with him. I'm tracking them down."

"Good girl. Tom, you help Eve with that."

Dymphna turned to Eve and mouthed, "Keep him out of trouble." Eve grinned, her neighbour really didn't think a man could be of much use compared to the powers of the average woman.

"We need to consider who else would have reason to kill her." Claudia said. "Even just to widen the field of suspects, away from poor Boyd."

"That's hard without knowing more about her," Dymphna pointed out.

"Well, while Greta gets on with that, you should tackle Ellen and Finn. And we need to know the truth about what happened in the states, before they came here."

"What would that have to do with anything?" Niamh asked.

"Ah. Remember what Boyd said. *"You're leeching off them, you're ruining everything -again.""*

"Oh. You think Dolores worked for them over there?"

"Almost certainly."

Ronan put up his hand. "Leave that to me. I can make official inquiries, get the full story. Dymphna can get the personal angle from Ellen and Finn."

Claudia nodded. "I've some digging of my own to do. Something has been bugging me ever since I saw her at the protest. No, I'm not saying anything til I double check. Just - leave it with me."

"Perfect." Dymphna turned to the detective. "Now, I take it the official cause of death was a blow to the head?"

Ronan hesitated.

"I can't give you that kind of information…" he said, slowly. "But for the sake of argument, if someone was hit with a single, devastating blow to the back of the skull – well, death could be instantaneous. And if they were holding something – like a torch in one hand, and a small gardening trowel in the other – you might or might not drop them. Or clutch them even in death A small, powerful torch and a red handled trowel…And hypothetically, if someone was crouched over, on one knee, digging or rooting at the ground and was struck from behind, that person would fall in a very particular way."

Dymphna and the others took a moment to digest this.

"Okay, then. Blunt trauma, while digging or searching for something. Write it down."

Ronan caught Tom's eye and shrugged.

"Better have them onside, than working against me," the look

said. Tom gave a nod of utter sympathy.

"It's getting late," Dymphna checked her watch. "I need to get ready, I'm off out to my daughter's for dinner. I'll be back around ten or eleven, Eve, if you're in need of company. Or Tom here could stay and mind you again. Make himself useful, eh?"

Niamh sniggered, then covered it with a cough as she read the expression on Eve's face.

"Good, good. I'll be off myself. Greta, I'll help you. Eve's cousin Claire is a civil engineer, she'll have the industry track on Dolores."

"Grand so, let me know what you find out. I'll put out a special edition of the podcast tomorrow evening – get the Goode Hunters on the scent."

The meeting broke up, leaving Eve and Tom alone finally. Ronan had gone to say a quick hello to his girlfriend, before returning to the station. He would be working night and day until the murder was solved, so any chance to catch five minutes with Margaret was welcome. Tom promised they'd look in on her, make sure she wasn't at a loose end.

"Why that pair don't just move in together, and be done with it, I don't know." Tom remarked.

"It's only been a few months, Tom. They won't want to rush it."

"I suppose. At their age, they have time on their side. But honestly, he's been mad about her for years. Dating was just a formality, they were as close as an old married pair for yonks before that."

Eve kept her head turned as she cleared away the cups and plates from the meeting. Try to sound nonchalant, she told herself.

"At our age, things are easier though – don't you think?"

There was a very eloquent silence from the other side of the room. Then a careful, "Yes. I think so. We know what we want. Comes from knowing who we are, I suppose."

"That's what I was thinking," Eve said quietly. "Like, when you're in your fifties – well, you don't feel you have time to waste, do you? You like someone, and they like you and…"

"And you just know!" Tom finished, eagerly. "I knew the first time I spoke to you – outside this house, when you said someone had been murdered! I thought you were so brave and capable and…well, I knew."

Eve turned to him, eyes shining, and – Bang!

"Oh for the love of -! Not again!" she shrieked, reaching for the back door keys. The sound of the last remaining shreds of her new garden fence being splintered to matchsticks filled the air, followed by the same, weird, lowering bellow she had heard the previous night.

Tom pushed her aside and said firmly, "Stay right here." He stepped out into the dark, Eve straining to follow the outline of him as he made his way down the path.

Without pausing to think – or doubt herself – Eve closed her eyes and followed him with a different sight. She could see the worried but determined frown on his face and the whitening knuckles on his clenched hands. She looked towards the fence and gasped – it was now reduced to two broken planks, hanging precariously from the frame, with a gaping hole in the middle. Tom paused, then stuck his head through the gap to look into the field beyond.

"Be careful!" Eve called out.

"It's okay," Tom shouted back, "There's nothing here."

To her horror, he clambered through and into the green

space, but reappeared almost as quickly, and repeated, "Nothing here!"

She went down to look at what was left of the fence. "This is ridiculous. Thank heavens I hadn't called Luke to fix it yet."

"I'll sort something out tomorrow," Tom promised. "But we need to get to the bottom of this. I know, the murder takes precedence but this is bizarre. I don't like you being here, while someone or something tried to kick its way into your garden."

"What if the two are connected?" Eve clutched his arm. "What if Dolores or her friend had some kind of machine, and when they used it, it damaged my fence? Something that breaks rocks, maybe – it's very hard to dig in that field, with all the rocks."

Tom looked at her doubtfully. "I don't know, love. Maybe. I can't think what, though. But I could ask around the builders, see if there's anything that would kick back like that. Maybe you're right."

"Well, it's that or some púca has taken a dislike to my garden," Eve said.

Tom laughed. "Well, when you put it like that – a machine of some kind sounds more likely. Your fence is destroyed, though. Look, let's leave it be for tonight and get Luke to take a proper look in the morning. Maybe we could use something to reinforce it…"

Eve let Tom natter on for a while, considering – and discarding – various ways of making the fence stronger. She tried to sense something, anything, at the site but nothing came to her. It was as if something had been there, something huge and strong, and then it was gone, pouf! As if it hadn't been there at all.

"It's been a long day," Tom finished, "I say we order a Chinese and worry about all this in the light of day."

Eve's stomach rumbled in agreement. "That," she said, "is the best idea I've heard all day."

Chapter 13

Claudia sat at her laptop and pulled up the membership files of the Irish Women's Brigade. Something about the name Dolores McIntyre tugged at her memory; in fact, the young woman's cheeky manner and brusque way of speaking was strangely familiar. She couldn't remember meeting McIntyre before, yet somehow she felt familiar.

She found what she was looking for, not in the lists of names but in a file marked "Annual Photographs." Every year since the Brigade had been founded, in the far off days of revolution and freedom fighting, each division had taken a group photograph of their members. Some of the younger ladies had used the lockdown to digitize the records, scanning them all from the oldest, sepia toned shots to the last ones taken on film in the eighties and nineties.

And there, in nineteen eighty six, was a group of thirty women of the Dublin 4 division; big hair, bright clothes, wide smiles. Claudia stared at the faces, recognizing a middle aged version of herself, in a purple blouse with huge shoulder pads. She smiled sadly at some of the older faces, long gone but not forgotten. Some of the young women were now the middle aged ones of the division, their own daughters proud junior members. And in the middle, a sullen dark-haired young woman, with her hair teased and hairsprayed into a high style and large plastic hoop earrings.

The late, rather unlamented, Dolores McIntyre.

***

Eve felt a bit like a stalker, loitering around the corner of Pine Tree Road first thing in the morning. She had to find a way to meet Ashleigh and her brother, without knocking on the door and dragging their mother into it. If they had a good explanation for being out and about at two a.m. she hoped to avoid getting them into any unnecessary trouble. And in her experience, teenagers clammed up the moment their parents got involved.

"I'm not sure what good explanation there could be, for being out at that hour in a field!" Dymphna had remarked drily when Eve explained her reasoning.

"You'd be surprised. Kids at that age, they do push boundaries. Maybe it was just a dare, or a bit of old fashioned rule breaking." Eve could recall catching Mairead in a park with her friends, passing around a bottle of purloined vodka from a parent's drink cupboard. "It doesn't make them bad kids, just kids making bad choices. Maybe Boyd doesn't want to land them in it."

Now, as she tried to keep warm in the freezing drizzle, she hoped she was right. If the teenagers admitted to being with Boyd, even if they were up to no good, it was an alibi.

Her patience paid off. Shortly before half eight she caught

a flash of red hair out of the corner of her eye, and turned to find the brother and sister walking towards her. The girl cast a quick glance her way, then did a double take.

"Oh. Hi." She offered a small wave. Eve reciprocated, trying to look surprised.

"Oh, hello. Nice to see you again." She paused, then added. "It's Ashleigh isn't it? And Sean?"

The girl looked surprised. Her brother, Eve noted, looked anxious.

"Yeah, that's us. I'm sorry, how did you know that?"

Eve shrugged. "Oh, someone mentioned you to me in my art class. Jenny, she goes to your school."

"Jenny Chan?" the boy's face cleared. "Yeah, she's in Ashleigh's year."

His sister nodded, but remained wary. "You were talking about us?"

"Well, yes and no. I mentioned getting a fright on the way home, described your lovely red hair and Jenny guessed it was you."

"Oh. Grand, so. Sorry about that, again."

"Oh, it's fine. It was my fault for day-dreaming. I hope you got enough hay?"

If she had asked them straight out if they had murdered Dolores Mcintyre, the pair could not have looked more guilty. Both looked shifty, dropped eye contact, shuffled their feet and then Ashleigh said with a defiant tone, "What hay?"

"The hay, you were collecting it for your school play?" Eve kept her face neutral, and the teens relaxed.

"Oh, yeah. Thanks. Yeah, we got enough."

"And when is it? The play, I mean?" Rearing two children through the teen years had taught Eve the art of gentle, but relentless, interrogation.

"It's – um, soon."

"We're not actually in it," Sean volunteered. "We were just helping out."

"Yeah. That's it. I mean, that's right. Not sure of the date, because…"

"You're not in it." Eve finished. "That's awfully nice of you both, to help out when you're not part of the play. Very… .public spirited."

Ashleigh kept her composure but her brother went bright pink.

"And….is it a nativity play?" Eve tipped her head to one side and smiled. "Only, I didn't think secondary schools put on nativity plays?"

"Oh. No. It's…um…"

"What does it matter?" Ashleigh matched Eve's smile. "Or were you planning on attending?"

Eve was impressed. For cool nerve, Ashleigh showed promise. Poor Sean on the other hand looked as if he wanted to run away. Their mother might not be very present on a day to day basis but she had obviously instilled manners into the kids and cheeking adults didn't come naturally to them.

"I might," She said agreeably. "If I've time…at the moment, the protest is taking up all my spare time."

Neither asked what protest, or pretended to be unaware – instead, to her surprise, the mention of the protest seemed to open doors.

"You're with the protest?" Sean asked eagerly.

"Yes, I'm – well, I'm one of the organizers, I suppose. From Bramble Lane."

"That's amazing. We think you're all brilliant."

"Thank you," Eve couldn't help but be flattered.

"Yeah," Ashleigh said, "It's so cool to see all you old folk out protesting, and the parents too. Even Mam went around for an hour."

"But especially you older ladies," Sean insisted. "It's so much harder for you, being out in the cold and standing so long. Everyone in my class was talking about it. Can't wait to tell them I met one of the Pensioner Protesters!"

"That's what everyone is calling you, in our school. We're all behind you. Wait til the weekend, you'll have all the senior years out, with placards."

Eve swallowed down the impulse to point out she was only fifty years old and in no way the same age bracket as the "Pensioner Protesters." Being part of the old bat group seemed to have currency with the teenagers.

"Well, hopefully the protest will continue – it's so hard to know what will happen now. That poor woman – awful thing to happen."

Ashleigh wrinkled her nose. "Eh. I know it's bad to speak ill of the dead and all, but – she was a horrible person. It's obviously sad for her family, and stuff, but I don't see why it should stop the protest. Wasn't she part of the building team? I heard she was the project manager. She would have ripped up that land and destroyed…things. Just for money."

Eve was used to the passion and occasional callousness of youth.

"I understand, but still – a human being lost their life. A person, murdered, in the middle of our community. It's important, very important, to find the killer. Otherwise, no one is safe. And worse, the innocent may be blamed, or at least have to live under suspicion. That can ruin a person's life."

Ashleigh narrowed her eyes. "Who? I mean, who is under suspicion?"

"Oh, you probably don't know him. They haven't started school yet. A young man whose family just moved here from the United States, Boyd Marrinan."

Sean went a sickly shade of greenish-white.

"Boyd? But – that's mad."

"Oh, do you know him? I must say, I agree with you. It seems highly unlikely to me. But he was there, in the field, around the time she died. A woman saw him and identified him. And he had a very public row with her, hours before."

Eve caught Ashleigh's eye, and added, "She saw two others with him, but Boyd won't say who they are, or why he was there."

The siblings exchanged a look, the boy stepping back to stand beside his sister.

"He must have a good reason not to say anything."

"Good enough to risk being arrested for murder? I find it hard to believe anything he was doing would be worse than murder. If he was up to a spot of vandalizing, or underage drinking – no one will be angry with him." Eve mentally crossed her fingers at the little white lie, feeling fairly sure Finn Marrinan would go through his son for a shortcut if he found out he was drinking. "Nothing is as bad as murder."

She had hoped that hearing it from an adult would prompt the pair to confess to whatever minor illegality had taken them to the field at two a.m. but she knew almost immediately her shot had missed its target. Ashleigh just looked exasperated and Sean shook his head, as if Eve had said something very stupid.

"If he was up to something, of course he would confess."

Ashleigh said. "I mean, if he's not talking, he must have a *good* reason."

Before Eve could digest this, the girl grabbed her brother by the shoulder and marched him past her, calling out, "Sorry, we're going to be late," as she went.

Eve stared after them. A good reason. What good reason could make Boyd willing to risk a murder trial and make two decent, nice kids willing to let him?

Chapter 14

Eve made a point of turning on the Christmas lights – both on the tree and over the mantelpiece – the moment she got home. This December was turning into a rather grim and worrying one, but she knew from long experience that sometimes you had to show Christmas cheer even if you didn't feel it yourself. She remembered night after night when Peter, her ex husband, would be out wining and dining staff and clients, staying out til the wee hours while she sat at home with the kids. Bedtimes were bad enough, Mairead in particular asking why Daddy wasn't home and when would they go see Santa and why didn't Daddy come to the school concert? Liam seemed to accept it more readily, which broke her heart in a different way. After the first no-show – Liam had been in the lead role, the Cowboy Who Saved Christmas – he never again allowed himself to hope that Daddy would turn up.

Mairead had kept fighting - and sometimes it seemed as if she blamed Eve for Peter's shortcomings. It was Eve who turned up to every school play or cheered her on at every basketball game and it was Eve who took the brunt of her daughter's anger and hurt when Peter didn't show up.

She understood it - which is why, whenever possible, she lavished time and attention on both kids. It was hard, trying to fill up the empty space.

But it was later, when the house was quiet, and the television full of silly films and Christmas specials, and her friends were out with their husbands at dances and parties and Christmas Carols in the National Concert hall – ah, now, that was the absolute worst. Nothing to keep your mind off how lonely you were and how little your own husband seemed to like you.

That was when she would light the tree – plain pale white bulbs, none of your vulgar, multi-coloured, flashing lights for Peter – and start wrapping presents, and write Christmas cards and send letters.

Eve looked around her little sitting room, and felt a surge of optimism. Sure, it wasn't how she had planned to spend her first December in Kimberly but this time, she was far from alone. She wasn't pretending to everyone that her marriage was perfect, her life was fine. Tom was as thoughtful as Peter was selfish, and her neighbours would come running if she asked them for anything.

So she lit her lights, adding a few to the garland on the mantelpiece, settled down to watch the latest episode of *Death in the Deise,* Ireland's favourite detective series, and put aside the problem of Boyd, and the Marrinans for the present.

In the house beside her, Dymphna was wrapping presents for her grandchildren. Her version of this involved sticking each gift in a gift bag, and stapling it shut, before tying a homemade tag to it. Each tag said *"With love, from Granny,"* and was guaranteed to bring a huge smile to each face. Granny Moriarty was known to give the best gifts. Even without being told, she somehow seemed to know what you really wanted. That pair of earphones your mates all had, but Mam said were a waste of money – they'd appear in a bright, glittered covered gift bag with that famous tag attached. Ditto, the trainers, or the make-up or the hair straighteners or the hoodie you craved. And the best thing was, the parents couldn't say a word, only roll their eyes and mutter about Granny being too generous and spoiling them.

Dymphna had seven grand-kids to date, and her eldest son was set to finally settle down, marrying a nice woman with three kids of her own. The wedding was in the following April but the names were already added to Dymphna's list and the three new grandchildren were about to be very pleasantly surprised by Derek Moriarty's mother.

A crow left the branch it had been occupying, its work as look-out done for the day. It rose into the air and circled over the crescent of houses in Bramble lane, over Margaret Fury's cottage where the teacher corrected her students' work, in front of the TV with a glass of wine. She glanced up from the copybooks, as an advertisement came on for engagement rings – the famous House of McDonald where generations of Dubliners had bought their tokens of love and marriage. Her breath quickened and her cheeks held a faint blush, just for a few minutes. Then laughing at herself, she returned to her work. But still, but still, the thought remains – it's not unthinkable, is it?

Tom MacDonagh was also hard at work, his kitchen table strewn with the intricate workings of an antique clock. His old life, the one before his wife died, had been spent buying, restoring and dealing in antiques and while no expert, clocks had always fascinated him. This was a special one, and the job important to him. He paused every now and then, the thought of young Boyd in a prison cell, or being interrogated, upsetting – but he placed his faith in Eve and her friends. "He'll be all right," Tom muttered at intervals. "We'll get him through."

Ellen Marrinan would have felt comforted if she had known the simple prayer Tom offered to the universe. The house was empty and cold, Melly sent to a friend's house for the night and neither of the adults caring to light a fire or even switch on the heating. How could they be warm, and safe, while Boyd was …but she couldn't bear to think of that. Instead, she turned to her husband for the umpteenth time and asked, "Do you really think they can help us, those old women?"

Finn looked at her and with a confidence only half feigned said, "Yes. Honestly, I do."

Ronan's house was empty, because Ronan was in work. He had a hard job convincing his superintendent to let him remain on the case, arguing that if he had investigated the death of a neighbour without compromise, he could surely investigate the murder of a complete stranger. His boss was a fair man and had to agree but was left feeling vaguely concerned that two murders in the one area, beside the same detective's house, looked a bit odd. Ronan also had a job convincing his partner that the case against Boyd wasn't a slam dunk.

"I don't get it!" His partner, Mike Cullen, complained. "You don't really know the kid, he was in the area, he threatened the victim…"

"Witnesses are adamant he didn't really threaten her, that it was in response to her threats."

"Ah…fine, maybe so. But he was there, he hated her – why are you so sure?"

Ronan sighed.

If he said "Because Dymphna Moriarty told me so," that would make Cullen think he needed a vacation from the pressures of the job. The truth was though, the old woman was like a barometer of human decency. If she liked someone, they were generally all right. If she disliked them – well, you ignored it at your peril.

He settled for, "It's just a hunch, I know. But he's only a young fella. Better make sure, okay?"

Cullen was one of the ones Dymphna liked. "I suppose so. Well, it's your call. Where do we start?"

They started with the background checks on Dolores and when they finally arrived in his inbox, courtesy of a Chicago Police Department clerk, they made for depressing reading.

"She was some piece of work, wasn't she?" Cullen shook his head. "I'm no longer surprised she was murdered, I'm only surprised it didn't happen sooner."

Ronan frowned at him, but had to admit, he had a point. Dolores had managed to stay on the right side of the law – just – but her name was linked to any number of unsavoury things. A building she was part owner of just happened to burn down, leaving thirty people homeless and Dolores the richer by several hundred thousand dollars. A planned development threatened to destroy a neighbourhood garden slash allotment in an inner city area and protesters found themselves targeted by thugs -car tyres were slashed, windows broken, people followed home. Despite their best efforts, the police had been unable to prove her involvement but in the time honoured fashion of police everywhere, a note on the file made it clear "no other credible suspect was being considered."

"They knew it was her," Ronan said. "And this one – an old couple threatened and harassed until they agreed to sell their house to her."

"Yet, for all that, she's got very few assets," Cullen said. "Look, thirty thousand in one bank account and a house in Chicago.

Valued around the eight-hundred thousand mark, but she was paying off the mortgage on it. Where did all her money go?"

Ronan nodded. "That's our first priority. Maybe she invested in something, maybe she gambled it all away…"

Cullen snapped his fingers. "Maybe she invested it in Marrinan's last project, the one in the states that turned their neighbours against them."

"Could be. Though, by all accounts, that was very profitable financially even if it was disastrous in other ways. Something's not adding up. Why did she follow them here?"

The other detective yawned and stretched. "Time to interview the Marrinans. Tomorrow. I'm wrecked."

Ronan agreed. "Let's take it up in the morning."

The detectives exited the station, glancing upwards as they did.

"The lights," Cullen pointed at the strings of festive lights strung across the street, and around lampposts. "When did they go up?"

Ronan laughed. "About three weeks ago. Some detective you are, not noticing that."

"I've been busy. I'm an important asset to this force, I'll have you know. Not some jaded auld plodder like yourself! It's nice though, isn't it? Finally feels a bit like the holidays."

Ronan grinned. "It is. Hey, we're going to organize a bit of a get together with the neighbours, maybe Christmas eve. Come along."

"Heh. I might just do that." Cullen took one more look at the festive display. "It'd be nice to have a bit of cheer, something to look forward to." Mike Cullen was a bachelor, not by choice. He had a happy, busy life but somehow, this year it got to him. He looked up at the bright lights, the festive decorations, and made a secret wish. Maybe the New Year would bring something new. He said goodnight to his partner.

As Ronan drove home through the city, the night turned frosty. Under a full moon, little creatures moved and hunted and the empty streets were peaceful and calm. He turned into Bramble Lane, cast a wistful glance at Margaret's house - it was far too late to disturb her - and froze as a fox crossed his path.

The animal turned amber eyes towards him, and they gazed at each other for a long moment. Then, with grace and effrontery, the fox turned his tail to him and padded off into the dark. Ronan grinned. Even an jaded auld plodder of a policeman could find magic in a Dublin city night.

And when all the residents of Bramble Lane were safely home, and their curtains drawn tight against the chilly night, something stirred in the dark field, among the briars and brambles - something large and strong, something the land welcomed but knew didn't belong. It ambled over to Eve's fence - or what remained of it - and stood, listening.

Chapter 15

"Welcome to Greta's Gory Truths! I'm your host, Greta Goode, and today we will be exploring…."Greta paused dramatically, "The truth behind the slaying of Dolores McIntyre!"

The script was one of Greta's best efforts, hitting the right note between sympathy for the victim and shocking revelations about her murky, and possibly criminal past. Long before the detectives had heard from their counterparts in Chicago, the Goode Hunters had come through with chapter and verse on the deceased. Greta's fan base stretched far beyond the confines of her native Dublin, and the podcast was a favourite of true crime aficionados, especially anywhere there was a community with ties to Ireland. Which was pretty much everywhere, thanks to centuries of emigration.

People tended to tell Greta things, without really knowing why they choose to confide in her. Maybe it was her twinkling eyes, or her *joie de vivre* or her almost hypnotic air of intense interest in their every word - which somehow transmitted itself through electronics, as if she was there with you in the flesh. But whatever the cause, Greta found that many an interesting, and highly confidential, tidbit came her way.

There were things in her files that the Gardaí would walk over hot coals to read.

The lowdown on Dolores wasn't top secret but it was explosive. People who had been fleeced in one of the building schemes, or invested in some development that went wrong, fell over themselves to let Greta know. Officials who had fallen foul of her temper, and even an old business partner, had all volunteered their stories and opinions. Usually, finding background on a victim or suspect took a lot of patient digging but the problem with McIntyre was the overwhelming volume of information. Trying to sift out the relevant and factual from the personal and biased, that was the hardest part.

Niamh had come through with a lot of information on Dolores' early career in Dublin, before she emigrated. Eve's cousin Claire remembered the woman very clearly and had plenty to say about her.

The sad fact was, none of the stories painted her in a good light. Greta liked to be fair to her subjects, and the idea of sharing damning information on the victim of a horrible attack didn't sit well.

On the other hand, it was hard to ignore the fact that Dolores had been a rotten, selfish person. She looked at just one of the many online conversations in the private Goode Hunters forum.

FleecedFromFallCreek *"She persuaded my husband to invest, all our savings, every penny! The building was supposed to be built in a year, and then we'd start seeing a return. But she hadn't even got planning permission yet...by the time the building went ahead we hadn't a penny left, we were struggling to pay for food, let alone bills. She ignored his calls, refused to explain the delay or tell us anything. The building did eventually go up, but his heart...she drove him into an early grave and I will never forgive her. And all I got out of it was a tiny percentage on top of the returned investment*

- it barely covered inflation."

Greta TheGoode *"Did you take any legal action?"*

FleecedFromFallCreek *"No, apart from sending letters from our lawyer while she refused to take our calls. Once the investment was returned, we had no recourse. It didn't matter that she didn't give us what she promised, the contract was worded so carefully just returning the barest extra on top of the initial monies put her in the clear. We had lived in poverty for five years, while she used our money."*

It was a similar refrain, as she worked through the emails and voice messages. Dolores and her associates had stayed just the right side of the law, albeit within a whisker of it at times.

"Our victim had a chequered past…" Greta rolled her eyes, knowing the phrase hardly conveyed the woman's legacy of deceit and broken dreams. "She was in many ways, a deeply unsympathetic subject to research. Many of my listeners have first hand experience of Dolores, and her business dealings. They have suffered stress, and disappointment and losses. It's important to stress, that no charges were every brought against Dolores, but it is fair to say, she was the focus of several investigations. But," and Greta's tone became severe, "She was a human being, who didn't deserve to die. She was a person, with hopes and dreams and I'm sure, some good points."

I couldn't find any, Greta reflected privately, but that doesn't mean she didn't have them.

"Goode Hunters, in the middle of a cold December night, here in the leafy suburbs of Dublin city, someone struck down and killed a woman, leaving her body in an empty field. We need your help - regardless of our opinion of the woman herself. A killer is at large, and justice *must* prevail!"

She waited a beat and then, in her everyday voice, continued.

"We have built a background sketch of her life, from Derry, to Dublin, then the United States, and finally back to Dublin. Anyone with additional information, contact me directly - all links are in my bio. So, let us start…Dolores Mary McIntyre was born in Derry city, in Northern Ireland, where she lived with her parents. An only child, she left Derry to study in University College Dublin, returning briefly to her native city when both of her parents passed away. She inherited a substantial property there, which she sold, using the proceeds to fund her first property deal back in Dublin. She was involved in the controversial development in St Enda's, where apartments built on badly drained land subsequently collapsed. Shortly after this, Dolores emigrated to the USA."

The next bit was tricky, Greta giving as much detail as she could without naming any names. Some of Dolores' business partners were litigious and the rest sounded downright dangerous. Greta weaved a compelling, but libel free tale of shady deals and bribes, harassment of anyone who stood in the way and failure on the part of the authorities to make a case against her or her associates.

"She was a clever woman, but even for Dolores McIntyre, there came a time when luck ran out. Last year, in a small town on the outskirts of Chicago, she met and partnered with a local developer who owned a strip of valuable land. She proposed a major development, one that would bring industry and prosperity to the area. It looked great on paper, but the reality was nightmare. A factory complex with an endless stream of trucks and heavy vehicles and pollution - it was the end of nature based tourism in the area."

No wonder the locals had turned against the Marrinans, she thought. Poor Boyd and Melly, the easy targets for everyone's frustration and anger. And no wonder Boyd hated Dolores…

"The fall-out was so huge, the man who sold her the land had to leave, and Dolores herself returned to Ireland. And this is where we find her, in the weeks leading up to the murder."

Greta switched off her mic and decided a cup of tea was called for. She had to tackle recent events without making Boyd or his family the target of more speculation. She was surprised the media hadn't already plastered his name everywhere - although as he was a minor, they were forced to be more constrained than with adult suspects. Ronan Desmond had called in a few favours too, and there was only fleeting mentions of Finn and Ellen, and their development plans for Bramble Lane. So far, no one had connected the unnamed "sixteen year old suspect," with Boyd Marrinan.

Munching on a slice of fruit cake, she went over the details in her mind and wondered how Claudia and the others were getting on. If anyone could supply Boyd with an alibi, it would make things much easier, and failing that - they needed more suspects.

* * *

Claudia called one of her favourite brigade members into her office and waved the photograph of a young Dolores McIntyre under her nose.

"Oh." Sahana Puri inhaled sharply. "Of course I remember her. Oh that woman!"

Claudia smiled. The Brigade kept meticulous records but nothing that could compare to Sahana's gift of recall. Not only would she remember names and faces, but give her a few minutes to think and she could tell you everything about the member – seed, breed and generation, as Claudia's mother used to say. She sat back and watched as Sahana turned things over in her mind, a frown of concentration on her face.

"She joined while she was in University – got in on the granny rule, if we're being honest."

The Brigade had quite strict requirements for membership, but daughters and granddaughters of members could claim the right to be admitted.

"Her grandmother, on her father's side, was Ermaline Dunleavy. Great woman, wrote the pamphlet on women's rights that got the Brigade banned in 1936. We were quite excited to have her granddaughter, if you recall. Maeve O'Leary wrote a piece on Ermaline for the Irish Express, around the same time." Sahana rolled her eyes. "Weren't we the eejits? That girl was nothing but trouble from the start. Of course, when you consider who her mother was…or to be fair, who her mother's family were…I suppose we shouldn't have been so surprised."

Claudia waited, but it was obvious that Sahana thought she should know.

"Who were they, then? We don't all have your memory, you know. I can barely remember what I did yesterday, never mind the scandals of forty years ago!"

"Oh. Well, she was a Gillespie. Her brother was the late Patrick Gillespie, the criminal. What did they call him - The Pigeon?"

Ireland's media had a bad habit of giving the underworld figures catchy nicknames, something Claudia deplored. She was fairly sure The Pigeon wasn't one of them though.

"The Hawk?" she hazarded a guess.

"Oh. Yes, of course, The Hawk. He was an odd one, too. His mother was a lovely woman, and his father was a decent enough man – but Patrick turned out to be a bad egg. And he dragged the rest of them down with him. Got his younger brothers involved – armed robbery, drugs, you name it. Nuala was the youngest, she married Dermott McIntyre and moved to Derry. Kept as far away from the Gillespie crime family as possible."

"But then Dolores moves here to study…"

"Exactly. She was all right at first…not someone you'd warm to, but all right. I was in charge of the Privates back then, and she was constantly angling to be promoted. Wanted to have a Corporal badge, and her not three months in the place. She was sly, too. She started reporting on other girls – really petty things. Remember how strict the Brigade used to be about girls drinking? The eighties were another country, young ones today don't know their luck. If you were caught in a pub, you'd get a reprimand and if you were caught drinking a pint, all hell would break loose."

The elderly ladies shared a conspiratorial laugh. The sexist rules that governed the Brigade in the past were long gone, but they had never been practical to implement, anyway. Many's the time she and Sahana had ignored them, reasoning that an organization set up to with the revolutionary spirit of the women of the 1916 Rising, had no business telling them what and where to drink.

"I told her to cop on to herself," Sahana said. "She was a right pain. But as I say, nothing major until her uncle started attending functions. Weaseling his way in, greasy little scalpeen. My mother had a saying she brought from India, *"Keep a hundred yards from an Elephant, but the distance one should keep from a wicked man is immeasurable."* It sounds pithier in Urdu but you get the gist. He was eyeing up the Brigade for one of his money laundering schemes, in my opinion. Of course, the Brigadier-General – your predecessor, Gobnait Dunne – sent him off with a flea in his ear. The man was in the papers every day with his antics, the last thing we needed or wanted was to have him photographed for the gossip columns at a Brigade function."

"I remember, now." Claudia grinned suddenly. "Sahana, pet, you're worth your weight in gold. You've sparked my memory back to life, so you have. Wasn't the Safe-Hands Security robbery around that time?"

Her friend stared at her. "Now you mention it – yes. That was the one where they got away with the gold, wasn't it?"

"Gold, yes. And valuables…I'm not sure what that means, but I presume jewellery and the like."

"Hang on." Sahana whipped out her mobile phone and typed furiously. "Ah! Gods bless the internet, Claudia. Look…"

An article popped up, detailing the famous heist.

"Thirty years since the State's most daring Robbery." Claudia skimmed through it, reading out the main bits.

"At least six individuals….believed to be linked to the Gillespie crime family…no charges ever brought. Fifteen million punts in gold, jewels, bonds and other items…the famous Quinn Coin Collection believed to contain rare, priceless coins." She looked up at Sahana. "The Quinn Coin Collection…wasn't Eimear Quinn one of ours?"

"She was. That was her husband Malachy's collection. She was Treasurer of the Brigade at the time, lovely woman. Her poor husband was distraught, he'd spent his life building that collection. It was on its way to be auctioned, for charity.

Poor man was ill, knew he hadn't long left and wanted to do something special with it."

"Of course! He was going to give the money to the Children's Hospital, wasn't he? And it was expected to fetch a huge amount of money. We held a fundraiser to replace some of it, after the robbery."

"That's it. Of course, it was nowhere near the amount he would have been able to donate but it did cheer him up. He was gone within the year. Eimear retired soon after, she's gone too now of course. But their daughter is a member, she runs the Meath regiment. And her daughter, too – she's a new recruit. This year's batch."

"I'm glad. It's important to see the tradition continue…but how strange it all is, isn't it? Dolores being so closely linked to the man who caused all that hurt."

"What are you thinking?" Sahana asked curiously

"Nothing…yet. But in my experience, very few things are mere coincidence!"

* * *

Dymphna rang the doorbell of Holly Cottage and waited. It took a few minutes but the door creaked open, just a little and a pinched, pale face peeked out at her.

"Melly! It's me, Mrs. Moriarty." Dymphna smiled at the child. "Let me in?"

Melly looked over her shoulder. "Mom says we're not to let anyone in…"

"Sure, give her a shout there and tell her it's me." Dymphna added encouragingly, "I come bearing cake."

Melly's eyes lit up and she eyed the large cake tin that

Dymphna was carrying. "What is it?"

"Christmas cake, the real deal. Made a month ago and fed with whisky. But you might prefer – " Dymphna popped the lid open so the girl could see the goodies, "my famous chocolate buns. Chocolate sponge, with chocolate buttercream topping and a sprinkle of chocolate shavings on top."

The door opened to its fullest width, Melly grabbed two of the proffered buns, and ran up the stairs, calling out, "Mom! Visitor!" as she went. She gave Dymphna a cheeky wink as she rounded the top of the stairs and disappeared from sight.

Ellen hurried out from the living room, her face thunderous. "Who the hell – Oh! It's you, thank heavens. I was afraid she'd let some reporter in."

"Don't be daft. Melly is a very clever young lady, she wouldn't do that. I'm afraid I bribed my way in though, with chocolate cakes. I hope you don't mind." As she spoke, Dymphna had made her way to the kitchen and was now busily opening cupboards and retrieving cups and plates. "Sit down there, Ellen," she instructed. "I'll make us all a nice cup of tea and we'll have a chat. Where's Finn?"

"He's out, with Boyd. They've gone to see the solicitor. That one you recommended, Ms. Warren."

"Ah, good. Claudia's daughter is excellent, they won't get one over on her. Well, I had hoped to talk to both of you but maybe it's just as well. You can talk freely, without Finn here."

Ellen bristled. "I can talk freely, even with my husband here. I don't like what you're implying –"

"I'm implying nothing." Dymphna peered at her, her sharp black eyes glittering. "I'm telling you. I've noticed how often you clamp your mouth shut, and bite your tongue. I'm not saying Finn is stopping you from talking, I'm saying you are stopping yourself."

Ellen opened her mouth, and then shut it again. A look that could be interpreted as relief crossed her face.

"I-I suppose you're right, in a way. It's just – I don't want to hurt Finn's feelings. All this has been terribly hard on him, and he's tried to do the right thing, all the way through. But everyone blamed him, even Boyd, and – oh, it all is just such a mess!"

Ellen had acquired a slight American accent during her time in the states, but as she talked, it faded away.

"G'won. Let it all out." Dymphna pushed a cup of hot tea and a plate loaded with Christmas cake towards her. "Sure, there's nothing you can tell an old woman like me, that could possibly shock me. I've heard it all, and done some of it."

Ellen giggled. "It's just so hard to explain. When we first met Dolores, she seemed really cool. Very professional, very clever. Finn and I started our business years ago, and we were successful. We built houses, schools, even got the contract to build a shopping mall. We were growing, but slowly. Then Dolores approached us about the land on the outskirts of town. Finn had bought it long before he met me, but it was in an area where building was discouraged. He had some idea of developing it for tourism, maybe a small hotel or Bed and Breakfast, with walks. But Dolores showed him – us, really – plans for a business park. What we'd call here, an industrial estate. She talked about the jobs it would bring in, the benefits to the town – and believe me, Mountain Heights needed jobs."

"It must have sounded exciting," Dymphna prompted.

"That's it! Exactly. We were excited. It felt like we'd be doing something good for the whole community, you know? I think – I think Finn thought he'd be a bit of a local hero. He loved that town so much, it was a chance to help it."

"But it didn't work out that way."

"No. First some of the community objected. Not a huge number of people, but they were very vocal. But they were the ones who were well off, middle class. We felt that they were just being selfish. What's that phrase? NIMBY. Not in my back yard. That's what it felt like. The ones who stood to gain employment, they were all in favour of it. Dolores said to leave everything to her, she knew the right people and was used to large scale developments. And she was. Before we knew it, we had planning permission. Then the environmental impact report was leaked, and people were furious. It was – damning. How we were granted permission to build there is beyond me, if I'm honest."

"Dolores had a knack for these things. All it takes is one corrupt official…"

"We didn't know, though. It never crossed my mind, not once. She was so *professional,* you see. And she knew everyone. She hobnobbed with Senators and Congressmen. I just thought, she knows the right people. It was naïve and self serving of me, I know. But when the report was made public, I was shocked. By then, though, it was too late. We were in so deep, and there was no way to pull out. We sold the land to Dolores but had to wait until completion of the project to get the money." She put her head in her hands. "What were we thinking? We trusted her, like absolute twits."

"She dazzled you. You're not alone, you know. She conned a lot of people."

"The thing is, she didn't exactly con us though. We made a fortune on the whole thing. More than we dreamed possible. But we sold out our town, in the process. The kids were devastated. Melly lost all her friends, and Boyd – well, Boyd got into a fight at school with a kid he used to be best friends with. That kid called Finn names and Boyd defended his dad. Nothing physical, but a huge screaming row in the middle of class. The school blamed Boyd though – the Principal was only dying for an excuse to have a swing at us. So we started to think about moving."

"Your mother is here, I understand?"

"She's in a nursing home, on Sydney Parade. She's not well, Mrs. Moriarty – Alzheimer's. She doesn't really know who we are, you see, but it seems to comfort her to have visitors. I was planning on coming to stay for a while, anyway, and then we started talking about Dublin and it seemed like such a good idea."

"It is a good idea," Dymphna said cheerfully. "Dublin is always a good idea. Aren't you living in the best little street in the city, with the nicest neighbours? Great decision, if you ask me."

"Neighbours who hate us," Ellen said gloomily. "I can't believe we made the same damn mistake again."

"Yes. About that – how *did* you make the same mistake? Like, the first time you can be forgiven for not knowing just what a creep Dolores was. But to do it all over again? That seems – unwise."

"Hah! Do you think for one moment we would have willingly got involved with that woman again?" Ellen snorted. "I hated the very sight of her. She tricked Finn, plain and simple."

And that was all she would say.

Chapter 16

Niamh sat down next to the teenage girl with the flowing red hair and smiled at her. The park bench was cold and hard, and December is rarely a good month to sit out of doors in Ireland, but the day was bright and clear, and she had carefully chosen as warm a scarf and hat as possible. She had spotted the girl from across St Enda's Park, her head down, slumped in the seat, red hair hanging loose under a knitted hat, and had made a beeline for her.

"Hello. Hope you don't mind me sitting here?"

The girl looked at her, a trace of resentment in her expression but she said politely, "Not at all."

"Thanks. Oh, it's nice to get the weight off your feet. Not that it's an issue at your age, is it? But when you get to be my age, that's when you really appreciate having a wee sit down. Toffee Chew?" Niamh thrust a bag of sweets at the girl.

"Gwon, love. Have one. It's a long day and the sugar will keep the cold out."

The girl hesitated, but accepted one. "Thanks," she mumbled.

"I love an auld sweet. Nothing like sitting and thinking and having a suck on a nice toffee. Answer to all life's problems, right there."

"Huh."

"You don't agree?"

"Some problems can't be solved that easily."

"Ah. Well, I'll concede that. But there's almost always a solution, if you can only see your way through the mess."

The girl turned her bright blue eyes to Niamh, her red hair catching the wintry sunlight.

"What if you can't see a way out?"

"Then you talk to someone else, get a fresh pair of eyes on the problem. You know who make great listeners?"

"Who?"

"Nosey auld women who sit on park benches!"

The girl laughed.

"I'm serious," Niamh continued. "There's a lot to be said for talking to strangers. And I am a very good listener. I also know how to keep a secret, which is a very rare skill. Plus, I have a lot of these lovely sweets to share."

There was a long minute of silence, before the girl stuck out her hand.

"I'm Ashleigh."

"Niamh. Pleased to meet you, Ashleigh. Now, want to tell me what's up?"

"I can't. Well, I can't tell you the details. It's - it's a secret, a really big one. An important one."

"Grand so. Tell me the gist of it then, the outline."

"Um. Okay. See, I have a friend. A really nice friend, he's very kind and he helped me and my brother with something. Something that was dead important to us. No one else would have done it."

"That's nice, pet. How did you meet this boy?"

"He's new, he only moved here. He was wandering around, and he looked lonely, so my brother -Sean - asked him would he like to hang out for a while. He just came and sat with us and we talked. He's not like a lot of the kids around here, he cares about the environment and stuff."

Niamh hid a smile.

"You liked him, then?"

"We both did. Anyway, we saw him a good few times after that. He made some other friends, but he still called round to us. That's nice, isn't it? Like, these new friends are dead popular and most people would choose them over us. But Bo- this boy wasn't like that."

"What went wrong, then? Did ye have a falling out?"

"Oh, no. Nothing like that. Like I said, he helped us with something and - and now he's in trouble because of it." She ended with something suspiciously like a sob and covered her face with her gloved hands. Niamh patted her shoulder and murmured sympathetically until she was able to continue.

"See, people think he did something awful but he didn't. And Sean and I know he didn't. But if we speak up, something awful will happen. Oh! It's so hard to explain."

"Not at all. Obviously, whatever he helped you with is top secret, and involves something very important. In order to clear his name, you would be betraying that secret. Is that right?"

"Wow. You really are a good listener. Yes, that's it. I can't let him be blamed for something he didn't do - but I can't help him."

"Hmm. It's a knotty one, I must admit. If it were me, I would try to find a middle ground."

"Middle ground?"

"Yes. You see, there's the truth - literally, factually, the truth. But then there's true enough, true to yourself, true friendship, reasonably true….*mostly* true. You're a clever girl. There are ways of telling the truth without telling all the facts. People don't really want all the facts, anyway. All those details, they're a bit messy. No, what you want is a nice simple truth - something people can understand."

Ashleigh frowned. "I think I follow you…"

"If it were me - and I'm not telling you what to do, mind! - I would take the relevant facts and see what I could do with them. For example - if you were with this young man, when he was supposed to be doing something awful, then you're his alibi. That's the important fact."

"I *was* with him!"

"Good. What's not so…relevant…is what you were doing at the time. All people need is a reasonable explanation. Say, you went somewhere to have a smoke - no, don't be annoyed! I can tell you don't smoke, it's just an example - where was I? Oh, yeah. You and your friend were having a cigarette, and you don't want to tell on him. You say you were there on a dare." "Lie?" Ashleigh shook her head. "You don't get it. I wouldn't just be lying to Mam, or his parents. This would be lying to the Gardaí."

"I would never tell you to lie." Niamh grinned smugly. "I'm telling you not to burden grown ups - even the cops - with information they can't understand."

Ashleigh looked long and hard into the elderly woman's soft brown eyes.

"Maybe you do understand," she said slowly.

"Maybe I do. In my experience, if the truth sounds too strange to be believed, it's cruel to impose it on people. Give them a nice, simple story to follow. Say you were there, for some silly teenage reason, and make sure Sean backs you up."

Niamh pressed one last toffee chew into Ashleigh's gloved hand and stood up.

"I'll leave you to think it over. If you need a hand, call round to my daughter, Eve Caulton. She lives at Kimberly Cottage, Bramble Lane. Oh, and you better find something other than hay for - your secret. I believe carrots are a favourite. And maybe a cookie or two. Anyway, call round anytime. In fact call around this afternoon - Eve will know what to do."

Ashleigh watched the old lady as she strutted through the little park, feeling slightly bewildered but strangely reassured. Then she called out, "Your daughter is Eve? Ms. Caulton? The artist?"

But Niamh just waved and continued on her way.

* * *

Eve was barely surprised to get home from her afternoon class and find half the neighbourhood in her house, scoffing their way through the biscuits and treats her mother had bought. The Marrinans, including the kids, were installed in the living room, with Margaret Furey and Tom. Claudia, Dymphna and her mother were at the kitchen table deep in discussion. There was no sign of Greta, but the back door was ajar, letting in a steady stream of icy air and letting out all the heat from the house.

"For goodness sake!" Eve rushed to shut the door properly, but Claudia protested.

"Greta and Ashleigh are out there!"

"I'm not locking it, just shutting it. Ye have the heat on full blast, but the door open. It's a waste of - Wait, who's out there?"

"Greta and Ashleigh. Honestly Eve, you just don't listen sometimes."

"Ashleigh?" Eve sat down in the one unoccupied chair and shook her head. "Why is Ashleigh in my back garden?"

"Turns out she's a huge fan of Greta's Gory Truths. Greta loves a fan. She's out there showing her top secret photos of some celebrity who is up for trial in the UK - according to Greta, it proves some alibi was faked, or something. Ah, here they are now."

The back door opened again, letting in another icy blast. Ashleigh, her eyes shining and her red hair peeking out from under a beanie, was chatting excitedly to Greta. Eve caught the words, "I never trusted her version of events…she definitely did it!" and frowned at Greta, who had the grace to blush.

"Greta, you shouldn't be pulling Ashleigh here into your conspiracy theories."
"It's not a conspiracy - it's a cover up," the irrepressible old biddy replied. "And it's not a theory either - it's a piece of evidence that I shall be sharing in an upcoming podcast."

"Not before my daughter looks it over," Claudia instructed. "You'll end up in a law suit one of these days, mark my words."

"I can't be sued if it's true," Greta replied smugly. She kicked Eve on the shin. "Get up there and let an old woman sit down. Your mother reared you better than that."

Eve got up, biting down the obvious retort. It was her kitchen after all, although her friends and neighbours seemed to think it was headquarters for a detective agency or the local residents association.

"Ashleigh, it's nice to see you," she said. "Everything all right?"
"Sort of. I met your mam earlier."

"Oh god," Eve winced. "What should I be apologizing for?"
"No, no. She was really nice. You're so lucky, having a mother like her. We had a chat and honestly she was so helpful. But she suggested I come and talk to you about - something. So I thought I would."

Eve glanced around. "There's not a bit of room - or privacy - in here. Come on, let's go for a stroll around the lane and chat. And if I can help, I promise I will."
She led Ashleigh through the living room, past the curious eyes of the Marrinans and Tom. As she paused in the hall to grab her hat and coat, Boyd followed them out, his face anxious.

"You're not leaving?" he asked Ashleigh.

"Just for a walk. I'll be back soon."

"Oh. Cool. See you then." He gave Eve a shy smile. "Thanks, Ms. Caulton. My parents say you're helping them, or rather, me. I do appreciate it."

"It's our pleasure. Although, you could be doing a bit more to help yourself, young man. Ashleigh, let's head out before it gets too cold."

She tried not to laugh out loud at the meaningful looks between the two young people. Boyd obviously thought the world of Ashleigh, and vice verse. And both had guilty secret written all over their faces.

"You and Boyd are good friends," Eve said, blandly. "He's a nice young fella."

"He is. Honestly, people think he's all moody and rude and stuff. But he isn't, he's just a bit…sad."

"I can understand that. He had to leave his home, and he had already lost the people he thought were his friends. It must have been hard for him."

"He has a hard time trusting people. I think that's why Sean and I get on so well with him."

"That's a rather sad thing to have in common," Eve said gently.

"Well, maybe not in exactly the same way but - two years ago, everything was perfect. Dad was - he was lovely. Funny, smart, and such a softie. Mam was fun too - she laughed all the time. Then one day, he died. Gone."

Ashleigh's tone was matter or fact, but her hands were tightly clenched. Eve said nothing, and they walked in silence for a few minutes.

"Anyway, yeah. Our lives just turned upside down one day. It makes you - different. People think I'm a bit weird. They think Sean is too quiet, too soft."

By "they," Eve assumed she meant, other kids. Until Ashleigh added, "My teacher called me an "odd duck," one day and everyone laughed. Miss Calthorpe. She was horrible anyway, but she seemed to step it up a gear when - when it happened. At first, we were out of school for a few weeks and when we went back, she made it her mission to make fun of me."

Eve bit her lip. *Wherever you are, Miss Bloody Calthorpe, I hope you're ashamed of yourself. And I hope you like it when you wake up and your car won't start and your dishwasher overflows, bad cess to you!*

She wanted to express sympathy but now Ashleigh had started talking, she was in full flow.

"Boyd got it, you know? He is so kind to Sean, took him under his wing. And we understood how it felt - how angry it made him, how sad. I just want you to know, he's not capable of hurting anyone."

"I agree. But - he was in the wrong place, at the wrong time."

"Your mam says you're investigating the murder?"

"Yes. We all are."

"And you can talk to Boyd's parents? You can explain stuff to them, for me? And the Gardaí?"

"Of course." Eve tried not to let her excitement show. "You have something you need to say?"

"I-I have a problem. I can tell you some parts of it. But I can't tell you the rest, I can't. It's not my secret to tell and someone could get really hurt if I told it. I mean, disaster level hurt not just a normal level. So, what I need to know is - can I tell the bits that are important and leave out the bits that aren't?"

"Let me guess," Eve grinned. "My mother suggested that you tell a plausible truth, rather than a problematic one?"

"Eh. Yeah."

"Oh dear. Mam has a very…flexible…approach to things. But she's right in some ways. It's better to tell what you can, and help Boyd, even if it means leaving out a few bits."

Ashleigh heaved a sigh of relief and hugged Eve's arm. "That's so cool. Now, can you help me think of a good… plausible truth?"

"Ah. Maybe you should tell me what you've come up with so far?"

"Sean and I were with Boyd, in the field. We never went anywhere near the back of Bramble Lane, though. We were down behind the shops, and behind my house. Boyd was with us from one until two thirty a.m."

"That's an alibi!" Eve clapped her hands.

"It'll prove he didn't do it, won't it?"

"It will - it will help, Ashleigh. The Gardaí will take it into consideration. But…someone coming forward, a friend, days after the fact and giving someone an alibi is a little suspicious. I warn you, they might not want to believe it. But it's certainly a help."

"So, what do I tell them - I mean, how to I explain that we were there at all? That's the bit I just can not be honest about, Ms. Caulton. I can't. I'm sorry."

"Never mind. I hope some day you can tell me, Ashleigh, because a secret that big is a lot for a person to carry alone. Still, right now -well, if you and Sean and Boyd had agreed to meet up, maybe on a dare, or to see what was happening with the protest…then it makes sense that you would climb back over your own wall, into your own garden, and maybe Boyd did too? Good. So, hoping there'd be some action at the protest, and egging each other on for a bet, ye hung around the edge of the protest, which is why that woman spotted ye. Then you went back to the far end of the field, near the shops and hopped over to your own side."

Ashliegh looked at her in awe. "That's really good."

"I had Niamh for a mother, don't forget. I had to come up with very plausible, convincing excuses."

"Did they fool her?"

"No, not once. But I kept trying."

They turned back towards Kimberly Cottage. Ashleigh looked as if a large weight was off her shoulders, and Eve was glad, but she was still worried. Would the Gardaí accept the story? It was the truth - for a given value of true - but it had to look very fortuitous, a last minute alibi.

She wondered what Detective Dempsey would make of it all.

* * *

"Never mind what Ronan says, I'll tell you what *I* make of it," Detective Cullen said, sitting in the kitchen of Kimberly Cottage a bare hour after Ashleigh had contacted Dectective Dempsey, "I think she made it up, to help her boyfriend."

"They're not dating," Eve said mildly. "Here, have another scone,"

Cullen took one, but shook his head firmly. "You won't get round me with baked goods. I'm not an easy touch like Ronan."

"Of course not," Eve murmured adding a generous dollop of cream and jam to his plate. "I knew you'd be far harder to convince. But honestly, I do think she's telling the truth."

"Hah. When Ronan told me this farradidle, he said the same thing. That's why I came around - someone sensible has to take a look at this so-called alibi. I should be at home right now - not that there's anyone there waiting for me. But I couldn't leave this until the morning. It's important to make sure this alibi is reliable."

"I completely agree. For Boyd's sake too - if it's not verified, it's no use to him."

"Yeah. Well. That too, I suppose. Any more cream? You make a nice scone, Eve."

"Thanks but that's one of Dymphna's." One of her "special" ones, Eve thought privately. Far be it from them to interfere with the majestic and solemn process of the law, but no harm in making Detective Cullen just a little more open-minded. Food cooked with love made people feel good. People who felt good, were better able to think well of their fellow humans. Cullen wasn't a cynic exactly, but he was inclined to be suspicious. A great trait in a policeman but awkward for other people.

"Tell Mrs. Moriarty thanks." Cullen pushed his plate away and patted his stomach. "I'd eat the lot of them, to be honest.

So, explain to me how you came to hear this convenient story? Are you close to her?"

"Ashleigh and her family are neighbours. Their house backs onto the green space, on the side opposite mine. Her mother works long hours - her dad died a few years ago. Ashleigh goes to school with some of my art students, she often knocks around the area with her brother Sean. We're not close, no, but I have come to know her recently. She's a nice kid."

"Nice kids fall foul of bad influences," Cullen growled.

"They do, Detective. I agree. But Boyd Marrinan isn't a bad influence. You should have seen him helping Tom the other day - worked like a Trojan. He's very nice to all of us. He's just a bit sad at leaving his home and a bit lonely here in Dublin."

To her surprise, Cullen nodded sympathetically. "We're a hard bunch to break into, the Irish. I've seen it time and again. We're friendly but it takes time to get to know people, we take a long time to open up. People think they'll move here and have instant best friends but we're a tribal lot at heart."

"That's it exactly. He finally made friends with Ashleigh and Sean, his first friends in Dublin. I bet he would have insisted on going with them, if they talked about creeping out to the protest in the middle of the night."

"Hmm. So you think, he was being protective?"

"Yes. I do. I think he wanted to make sure they were okay, to help them. Then when he was arrested, he thought Ashleigh and Sean would be in awful trouble so he wouldn't give them away."

"The mother, is she aware the kids are running around the place?"

"She's a hard-working single parent," Eve said reprovingly. "She doesn't have eyes in the back of her head and they're not little kids. They've never done anything like that before."

"Okay." Cullen shrugged. "I'm not saying I'm convinced but I suppose, it's not beyond the realm of possibility. We'll take it on board."

"That's wonderful, thank you!" Eve couldn't hide her delight.

"Wonderful, for you," the Garda sighed. "We're left back at square one."

"No other suspects?"

"More like too many. The woman made enemies left, right and centre. If we traced the movements of every one of them, it'd take six months. Maybe someone followed her from the States, maybe there's someone she annoyed here in Dublin." He rubbed his face wearily. "So, we've our work cut out for us."

"Did Ronan tell you we saw Dolores out in the field the night before the protest?"

"He did. Why? You think there's some significance to it?"

"I - I'm not sure. Maybe it was just her checking on electricity cables and pipe lines but it didn't feel like that. She didn't see us, you know, so she was talking to her friend very freely. I remember them mentioning a rock, with markings on it."

"Which could be a marker for cables," Cullen pointed out.

"Yes. I know, I'm sorry - all I can say is, it's a feeling. I think they were up to no good out there."

Cullen eyed her narrowly for a moment. "Okay. I'll take what you say on board. After last time, I'm not going to discount anything you or the auld women say - even if it's just a hunch. But right now, we have no real suspect other than young Marrinan and that needs to change. Bring me something, anything, that puts another in the frame and I'll deal with it.

But I can't write "she had a feeling," on the paperwork, you understand."

Eve nodded. "I get it."

Cullen gave her a brisk nod. "I'll take my leave, then. Be careful, Eve, if Boyd really is innocent - there's a killer on the loose."

Chapter 17

The following morning, Tom called around early, bearing croissants, pain au chocolat and coffee.

"You looked tired last night," he said shyly. "I thought it might help to start the day with a bit of company and a treat."

"I don't need any more treats," Eve answered, patting her waistline ruefully. "But, sure, it's nearly Christmas. I'll have half of each."

Half an hour later, all that remained of Tom's breakfast feast were crumbs and they both agreed to start a good, healthy diet - in the new year, obviously. By unspoken consent, both avoided any talk of the murder, instead making plans for Eve's art class Christmas party, and other happy topics.

"I really have to get ready," Eve said eventually. "I'd sit here all day chatting to you, I really would, but there's things that won't do themselves."

"You go on, love, I'll tidy this mess away. I'm off to my brother's today, he needs help with his attic. Leak in the roof, it'll take all day to move stuff so the roofers can repair it. I'll be back around ten. If you're up, text me."

Eve went upstairs, getting ready for the day to the pleasant, domestic sound of Tom clearing plates and washing up. It was nine o'clock, time for the news headlines, something Tom rarely missed.

"Stick on the news for yourself," she called down to him. There was the theme music of the RTE news programme, the murmur of the announcer's voices - and then a sudden upturn in the volume.

"EVE!" Tom bellowed up the stairs, causing her to drop her hairbrush in fright. "There's a fella from the University on the telly, and he's talking about the protest!"

She ran down the stairs with more haste than grace. "Rewind it there, Tom."

"It's live, I can't rewind it."

Eve rolled her eyes and grabbed the remote. "It's a smart TV, just press rewind and …there we go."

The news at six rolled back to reveal a headline banner, "Environmental expert speaks out against protest," and the solemn face of Dr. Murray, Environmental Studies, Leinster University," appeared on screen.

"Big shiny head on him," Tom grumbled.

"Hush. Let's hear what he has to say."

"While I sympathize with locals, this protest is highly misguided." He looked directly into the camera with a painfully sincere smile, that Eve was willing to bet he practiced at home in the mirror. "Now, I know my esteemed colleague Professor Blennerville has allowed herself to be drawn into this display – for which she has received a lot of publicity - but I feel it is only fair to put the other side. In a city crying out for housing, we cannot turn the development of every patch of land into a cause célèbre! Especially in an affluent area, already well serviced with parks and amenities. The simple truth is, there is no major environmental reason why this small field cannot be developed for housing."

He beamed at the young reporter, who smiled sweetly in return. Then she asked, in a tone that heavily implied she wasn't at all impressed with him, "You seem to think that area is entirely affluent, Dr Murray. In fact, like most areas of Dublin, there are plenty of ordinary people, ordinary workers, struggling to pay rent and mortgages."

"Oh, yes. Of course, of course. But the fact remains, there are two large parks –"

"There are two large parks in the greater area, Doctor. If you stretch the definition of "local" to breaking point. Only one is within walking distance of the actual site in question and even at that, it'd be some walk. This ground was ear-marked for a playground, for local families. And a skate-park for teens. Instead a small enclave of ….*affluent* housing will be built on it."

"Well – well, that's a minor point in comparison – my main point was that there is no pressing environmental reason not to develop it."

"Apart from the fact that we lose a green space, the trees that will be cut down, the plants that will disappear? There are wildflowers growing there that are vital to the plan to support bees and pollinators in the city – surely we can't afford to lose them?"

"Young lady, you must understand, environmental needs have to go hand in hand with the needs of society. Housing –"

"But you're not a lecturer on housing, are you? Or economics? Your field is the environment and you're the only one advocating for less green space, rather than more – why is that?"

Murray spluttered some answer that was received with a frosty smile.

"Thank you, Doctor. That was Doctor Murray, Leinster University giving his very unusual opinion on the protest in the Merrion area against a proposed development. This is Catríona Maguire, over to you in the studio…" the segment was replaced by the regular news desk, and a segment on the cost of Christmas dinner.

"Well, that wee girl gave him a right pasting!" Tom crowed, rubbing his hands. "He wasn't so cocky by the end, was he?"

He glanced at Eve, who was standing stock still, her gaze still riveted on the screen.

"Eve? The reporter was great, wasn't she?"

"Yeah. Of course she was, Tom. Did you not notice the name – Maguire? That's Sergeant Jo's sister. Greta's grandchild. Murray never stood a chance."

"Oh. I didn't know Greta's granddaughter was on the telly. Isn't that something?"

"Yeah. Know what else is "something?"" Eve turned towards him. "I recognize that Murray fella. Well, I recognize his voice. That's the man who was with Dolores, out in the field, the night before the protest!"

* * *

Ronan Desmond was interested, if not overly moved, by Eve's news. "Well, it's something to look into. Any lead that doesn't involved Boyd Marrinan is worth pursuing."

"Boyd?" Eve felt a pang of alarm. "I thought ye accepted he hadn't anything to do with it?"

"Eve, it's not that simple. He has an alibi, of sorts, but – well, he and his friends were at the scene around the time of the murder. If the powers that be decide he's a viable suspect…"

"He's not out of the woods yet." Eve finished. Ronan was only reiterating what Detective Cullen had said, but part of her had hoped the older man was being cautious.

"Ashleigh coming forward helped, no doubt about it. But we need to figure out who did it, or he'll be under a cloud for the rest of his life. Everyone will say he did it, even if he's innocent."

"I hadn't looked at it quite like that," Eve admitted. "But we'll get there, Ronan. You and Cullen will crack this."

With a little help from your friends, she thought as she ended the call. What to do next? The protest was still ongoing, albeit with a skeleton crew. Work had been suspended, with Finn and Ellen otherwise occupied. But Jenny and her friends had taken the University students under their wing, and were often down helping with the environmental survey. They were still optimistic that some rare plant or mushroom would pop up, and stop any talk of ripping up the land.

Perhaps she could chat to some of the students, get a sense of what Dr. Murray was up to. In her experience, young people were very shrewd judges of character when it came to certain things. A teacher that was nice to parents, but mean to kids, a lecturer who made snide remarks or said one thing while doing another. Making her mind up, she wrapped up and walked briskly to the site's main entrance.

Several of the protesters greeted her, among them Mags Phelan, the young mother she had met while looking for Ashleigh and Sean Conlan. The toddler, Ciarán, was fast asleep in his buggy and his mam was taking the chance to chat to adults and sip coffee. Her face lit up when she saw Eve.

"Hiya! How's the artist?"

"I'm grand, thanks. How are you? How's the wee man

doing?"

"Oh he's bold as brass," Mags said proudly. "Not a bother on him. Hey, have you thought any more about art classes for parents and kids?"

"To my shame, I haven't. But I do love the idea, and I will run it past the community centre committee, I promise. It's just been a hectic few weeks."

"Totally understand. This time of year is mad, isn't it? All the running about, present buying, food shopping…I sometimes wonder why we do it to ourselves. You know, I watched a video the other day and this woman said she started making homemade gifts, and only bought the minimum. I don't know if I could go that far but it makes you think, doesn't it?"

"It does. I used to live in a large house, with big expensive decorations, new ones every year, and no shortage of money. It was lonely. I wouldn't go back. Now, once I've a few decorations up and a present for everyone to open, I'm as happy as a pig in muck."

Mags laughed. She had a big, throaty laugh and a smile that reached her eyes, crinkling them.

"You're a wise woman. I used to party all December – used to party from November, if I'm honest. And it was great fun but now we have this little monster, Damian and I don't miss it. You know, a night out with my friends coming up to Christmas and I'm happy."

"Priorities change," Eve agreed. "Have fun, never stop that. But appreciate the small things, too. Listen, here's my card. My daughter had them made up for me, it has my email and stuff on it. You drop me a line when you get a moment and I'll get those classes set up."

Mags took it with a delighted smile. "Perfect. So are you

here to wave a banner with us?"

"Not right now. I've done my share of banner waving, and I'm sure I'll do more. But I was hoping to catch up with some of those students from the university."

"Oh, they're over on the far side, see that woman in a green jacket?" Mags pointed towards a tall, slim figure in a bright green jacket, who was bent over talking to a young man who kneeling down. They seemed to be examining a patch of land with great interest.

"That's Professor Blennerville."

"Oh! I didn't realize she came here herself. That's the very woman I need."

Eve took her leave and trudged across the hard, bumpy land with as much speed as she could without turning her ankle in a rabbit hole. As she approached, the Professor glanced at her, a smile of inquiry on her face. She was a woman in her fifties, with short dark hair, large brown eyes and an expressive, attractive face. She waved a gloved hand at Eve – the glove was originally green and woollen but was now streaked with dirt and soil – and pointed at the ground.

"Watch your step," she said, "We have a patch here that might be important."

"I'm glad to hear it. You're Professor Eithne Blennerville? My name is Eve Caulton, I'm a local resident. Actually, that's my house right there."

Eve pointed out the remains of her fence, still inexpertly boarded up. "It doesn't usually look like that, something battered it last week and I haven't had a chance to get it fixed. I'm one of the organizers of the protest…"

"Please to meet you." The Professor went to shake hands, looked at her gloves and stopped herself.

"Sorry, you don't want to be covered in muck. I'm afraid this is messy work at the best of times. In Winter, it's either pure mud or rock hard, frozen ground."

She laughed merrily, as if delighted by the vagaries of nature.

"I'm afraid we haven't good news for you yet, but I remain hopeful. This piece of ground has been undisturbed for a long time, hasn't it? All kinds of interesting creatures making their home here."

"If you could find something, anything, that would be great. We don't want to win this fight only to have another developer swoop in and build something here."

"I agree. We'll keep our fingers crossed and our eyes open – Marcuso! Don't use that trowel, you'll damage the roots – Sorry, you have to keep an eye on them. Great bunch of kids, but they can get carried away."

"We're grateful to have them. And you, you've been so kind to get involved."

"Oh, anything for Claudia Warren," the Professor said enthusiastically. "That woman is the reason I stayed in college, back in the day. My parents were financially embarrassed, as my dad used to say, and I was lucky they could scrape together enough for my undergrad degree. A masters - that was out of the question. I desperately wanted to, but thought I'd have to do a teaching degree."

"Ah. The H-Dip." Eve smiled. "Lots of my friends did that, it was almost the only career open to a lot of people after a Bachelors in Arts. I was in art college, but I remember them bemoaning it."

"I was in Science," Professor Blennerville said. "It was the same for us, by and large. Anyway, my mother was a Brigade member, and I was a junior member – more to please her than anything else. Claudia was one of the senior ladies even then. She moved heaven and earth to get me the funding. That was before the EU grants, too. I did a masters, then a PHD and now, here I am. Up to my armpits in brambles, trying to find a rare plant or an endangered species."

She laughed again and Eve joined in. She was a nice woman, she decided. Someone you couldn't help but warm to. She noticed the students near them, still on their hands and knees, listening to the Professor's story and exchanging admiring glances. It was clear she was both popular and respected – not an easy combination to achieve.

"Claudia is certainly an force of nature. She's one of my mother's best friends and believe me, I've seen her in action more than once."

"She is great, isn't she? Tolerates no nonsense, takes no prisoners…"

"Speaking of nonsense," Eve seized her chance. "I saw a colleague of yours on the news talking about the protest…"

"Murray." Eithne Blennerville said flatly. "Don't. He's an embarrassment. The man doesn't seem to engage his brain before he opens his big mouth. Wasn't that young one interviewing him only brilliant?"

"Catríona Maguire. Yes, I think we'll see a lot more from that young woman. But yes, Murray seems to hold unusual opinions for an environmentalist?"

"How he got that gig is beyond me. Of course, there's always careerists in academia – they play the game, until they get themselves into a position of power. Cosy up to the right people, publish in the right journals. But even allowing for that, he's an outlier. He was a contemporary of mine, in college, and he was at best an average student. But he came from a well known family."

Eve sighed. "Well known family," like "good family," was a time honoured Irish euphemism for well-connected, rich and powerful.

"Daddy was rich, then?" she asked.

"Rich, yes. But by well-known I mean…how to put this? Notorious."

"What?"

"His dad was a major player in the criminal underworld. Known to the Gardaí, as the saying goes. You must remember back then, the feud between that Hawk guy on the Southside of Dublin and your man from the North side? The Undertaker, he was called. Severe looking, po-faced thug of a man."

Eve did recall it. Anyone of her age, who was from Dublin, would remember it. Gillespie, the Hawk, who had ruled the south side. Claudia had mentioned that, hadn't she? Dolores McIntyre was his niece. And now Murray was the son of the Undertaker, the ruthless gang boss whose reputation was fearsome.

"The Gardaí broke those gangs though, in the nineties, didn't they?"

"Broke them…yes, I suppose so. The Criminal Assetts Bureau in ninety-six finished them off as any kind of major power. But Murray, the Undertaker and that Gillespie one, they never stood trial or anything. They just faded into the background, with their ill-gotten goods."

She smiled at Eve's face. "You're wondering how an environmental studies professor knows all this about the seedy underbelly of the city? You should listen to Greta's Gory Truths, it's a brilliant podcast. What that woman doesn't know about crime in Ireland isn't worth knowing. She should be in charge of the Gardaí, honestly. She'd soon sort them out. She's some woman for one woman."

Eve stifled a slightly hysterical laugh at the thoughts of Greta Goodie, Garda Commissioner, ordering the likes of Ronan Desmond around.

"I know Greta," she replied. "And she is indeed, some woman."

"You *know* her!" the Professor breathed. "Oh, holy night. Really? I'd give my eye teeth to meet her."

"You've probably seen her around, at the protest," Eve replied. "But you know what? You come to mine for tea this evening and you'll meet her properly."

The other woman surprised Eve with a bear hug.

"I will, give me your exact address. That's brilliant, now. I can't wait."

"And if you don't mind, maybe she could pick your brains about Murray? And Claudia will be there too."

"Seven o'clock suit you? I'll be there."

Eve hurried home, texting both Greta and Claudia on the way. If previous evenings were any predictor, the whole of the neighbourhood would probably be in her kitchen anyway when she got home, with or without invitation. But experience had taught her that the one time she expected them, would be the very day they didn't turn up. She made sure they were coming, then paused to think.

There were so many bits of information, all floating around. Dolores' past, the Marrinans and their story. Now, Murray and his involvement – it was time to gather it all together and see what they had. But it was also very close to Christmas and she had presents left to buy. There was only so much the local shopping centre had to offer and a limit to how many handmade items she could make. Her paintings made great gifts for other people but her own family and friends were already proud owners of a Caulton original. It was time to brave the city centre, and grab those last bits and pieces, if she didn't want to be wrapping gifts on Christmas Eve.

Another thing Peter, her ex husband, had never wanted to do, Eve thought as she boarded the Dart, Dublin's light railway servicing the areas as far out as Monkstown and Glenageary and into the heart of Dublin. Peter had resisted any attempts to go gift shopping in December, preferring to leave everything to Eve. "It's too crowded," he'd complain or "All this fuss for one day, it's ridiculous." One year, she had tried to bring the children to see the lights being turned on, Mairead's favourite boy band doing the honours. Peter had agreed, but then baulked at the last moment. "The rugby is on," was his excuse, followed by "and it'll just be full of plebs."

Anyone who wasn't Peter or one of his well-to-do friends, were "plebs," Eve recalled. She shuddered. How had she let him away with it for so long? But then, when you're in it, you don't see it – her mother's words.

It had therefore been quite some time since she had gone into town this close to the holidays. It was already twilight, the dark December afternoons making themselves felt. Ireland in summer basked in long bright evenings, until eleven o'clock at night at the height of the season. In Winter the evenings took their revenge, arriving early in the day and stretching far into the morning. The upside of this was that the city lights stood out, twinkling and bright, long before the shops closed. A huge tree had been placed outside the main entrance to St Stephens Green park and the length of Grafton Street, with its famous shops and cafes, was festooned with garlands of golden bulbs and chandeliers that could have graced a fairy-tale ballroom. Added to this were the individual decorations in each shop window, from the traditional gold, red and green to the avant garde, modernist décor of the cutting edge boutiques. Somehow, it all worked.

And yes, it was busy, but cheerful and bustling. A ukulele band with singers played carols and collected for charity, groups of schoolchildren skipped past her in crocodiles on their way to the Gaiety Pantomime matinee, an eagerly awaited school treat. Young mothers eyed up the cutest, most ridiculously impractical outfits for their babies and toddlers, while self-conscious young men approached perfume counters, asking for advice. Eve made short work of her shopping list, then happily wandered around, soaking up the atmosphere. Just as when she had stood on the land and felt its heart, the hoary old soul of the ancient city opened up to her – and she felt its love and energy.

It was a tired but happy woman who made her way home, parcels and carrier bags in both hands. Even the sight of her mother, waving from the living room window of Kimberly Cottage, couldn't ruin her mood. Besides, she had become resigned to Niamh's cavalier use of the spare key she had left with her, for "emergencies." The Irish Mammy didn't recognize boundaries, not ones of Niamh's generation anyway. Eve hoped she was better with her own kids.

"Mam." She dumped her bags on the kitchen table and looked around. "Dymphna, Claudia, Greta, Ronan, Tom, Margaret… How nice of you all to visit."

Ronan grinned. "Don't blame me. Your mother and Dymphna insisted – apparently we need to catch up on developments."

"We do," Eve conceded, "but does it always have to be in my kitchen? Have you no biscuits in your house? Does Margaret not have any, or indeed, Dymphna."

"But you're the leader of the band," Ronan said. Eve blinked in surprise.

"I am not. Have you met Dymphna Moriarty?"

"I have. And yes, she's in charge, generally. But when it comes to investigations, you're the head honcho."

Eve wasn't sure whether to be alarmed or flattered.

"I suppose you're all here now. Make yourselves useful, Professor Blennerville is coming for tea at seven. Greta, turns out she's one of your unhinged fans. She's dying to meet you, so make a fuss of her. We owe her a lot."

Greta preened, her round face dimpled in smiles. "One of my Goode Hunters? Always happy to meet a fan."

"The rest of you, tidy up and help me. The woman is expecting us to feed her and it's nearly half six already."

Many hands make light work, and the house was soon in order. She plugged in the Christmas lights, and realized there was a new addition to her display, a twelve inch high reindeer with a glowing red nose.

"Isn't it gas?" Niamh saw her looking at it. "Ashleigh dropped it around. Said she saw it and thought of you."

Eve stared at the reindeer, something tickling away at the back of her mind. Before she could grasp whatever it was, a knock at the door announced Tom's arrival, accompanied by a smiling Professor Blennerville.

"I found this lady wandering the crescent," Tom said, "She claims you invited her for tea. I tried to warn her about you lot, but she insisted."

"Shurrup. You're so welcome, Professor."

"Please, call me Eithne. Even my students call me Eithne, to be honest. Unless they're in trouble!" She laughed that merry laugh, that made everyone smile. Once again, Eve was struck by her youthfulness, which had nothing to do with physical appearance and everything to do with a lightness of soul and heart. It was infectious.

"Eithne. This is Tom, ignore everything he says. He thinks he's fierce funny. This is my mother Niamh, my neighbours Dymphna, Margaret and Ronan and our friend Claudia. And this," Eve gestured with the air of introducing a celebrity or a favourite circus act, "this is the one and only Greta Goode."

A beatific smile crossed the Professor's face and she grasped Greta's outstretched hand in both of her own.

"Oh. My. God. I've been listening to you since the podcast first started. I may be your biggest fan, honestly. I have the sweatshirt, the hoodie, the coffee mug – look!" Eithne fished in her bag and produced a sleek, black insulated thermos mug with the words "Greta's Gory Truths," emblazoned across it in blood red. "I can't believe I'm finally getting to meet you!"

Greta smiled graciously, tucked her arm through Eithne's and drew her into the kitchen, murmuring, "How nice, tell me - what precisely do you admire most about my podcast?"

Tea was eaten with gusto, the guest of honour sitting at the table with the older ladies and everyone else, including Eve, perched here and there. At first the conversation revolved around the true crime podcast, but eventually it turned to the professor's work and her opinion of her colleague, Dr. Murray.

"It's annoying of course, when he goes on national television to criticize me." Eithne shook her head. "I won't pretend I like the man. For an environmental expert, he's very pro ripping up the environment. He's a bit of a hired gun, to be honest.

When some company wants an "expert" to tell everyone they should be allowed to plough through endangered plants and important breeding grounds, up pops Dr. Declan Murray."

"My Catríona put him in his place," Greta helped herself to another slice of cake.

"She did, the wee pet. I was delighted, not going to lie. He's an embarrassment to the department. And as I was telling Eve, he is connected to very unsavoury people."

The others were agog as Eithne explained Dr. Murray's family history, especially his links to the infamous crime boss. Eve, already aware of the facts, allowed her mind to wander. After such a relaxing afternoon her brain had had time to turn over all they knew so far. Claudia had filled her in on Dolores' time in the Brigade, her family link to the Hawk, Gillespie and the tangential connection to the scandalous SafeHands Security robbery. Was any of this relevant, or did the answer lie in the recent past – her antics in the United States and her insistence on a partnership with the Marrinans, here in Dublin.

Or, she sighed, was it the woman's unpleasant personality that had prompted someone to lash out?

Chapter 18

The room was warm, between the blaze in the fireplace and all the people crowded in. Eve felt her eyelids grow a bit heavy, the cheerful babble around the table adding to the soporific effect. Claudia was telling everyone about Dolores' past, now, and she felt Ronan stiffen beside her at the news. But try as she might, she couldn't bring herself to tune in to the details or join in the conversation.

"This is silly," Eve thought, "I'm standing up, I can't possibly fall asleep."

She thought perhaps if she went outside, opened the back door and stepped out into the cold night air, she might wake up. And there she was, in the middle of the garden, but the air was strangely warm - where was the cooling bite of the winter? She could still hear the chatter and laughter, but now she was peering over the battered fence, although she couldn't remember climbing up on the garden furniture, and there was no way she had a ladder - had she? Her thoughts were jumbled and slow, and things seemed to be happening too quickly to grasp. She distinctly heard Tom's voice, saying something about Dolores, her past in the States, her lack of empathy…something moved in the darkness, in the far reaches of the field, which looked bigger than she remembered. In fact, it looked immense, more like the plains and hills of the Curragh of Kildare than a piece of green space in a city suburb. Against this dimly perceived landscape, the thing that moved was still huge, a lofty head and majestic flank and if she leaned forward, further and further, she might be able to see it clearly - and a tug on her arm brought her back, back to the kitchen and the present.

"You were away with the fairies," Dymphna remarked drily, from where she was sitting at the table. Eve stared at her, stupefied.

"I think I nodded off," she whispered. No one else seemed to have noticed.

"You were away," Dymphna repeated. "What did you see?"

"I was…I thought I was in the back garden, looking over the fence. But it all looked different, bigger. There was something…some big creature, but I couldn't see."

"You almost toppled over," Dymphna murmured.

Eve rubbed her eyes. "Everyone, I'm absolutely beat. Can we move into the living room? Bring in the kitchen chairs and we'll all have somewhere to sit."

The living room was scarcely less warm than the kitchen but as it had the benefit of more space and comfy chairs, at least she wouldn't be falling asleep on her feet. Dymphna gave her arm a squeeze as she passed, and muttered, "Let's deal with the here and now, and leave the rest til later."

Dymphna was right, Eve thought. Time enough to worry about strange creatures wandering the area after they cleared Boyd's name. She dragged her attention back to the eager chatter around the living room.

"I know Ellen claims that Dolores tricked Finn into taking her on as a partner, but to be honest I just don't buy it." Greta stabbed the air with one bony finger, her shiny red nail varnish catching the light as she emphasized each point. "One! He knew her reputation by then. Two! He knew it would upset Boyd. Remember how angry the kid was, shouting at his Dad, long before the murder? Finn had to know that would be the final straw for his family. Three! From what Niamh and I discovered, Finn's company – Marrinan Holdings – listed two directors initially. Just Finn and Ellen, with Ellen acting as company secretary. Then two months ago, just before the planning permission was granted, Dolores hops on board. Something happened to change his mind about her."

"Maybe they couldn't get planning without her? She's been known to circumvent the normal channels. If Finn had everything tied up in this development and it looked like the permission would be refused…he might have decided to let Dolores do her thing." Eve suggested.

"It's possible," Greta conceded. "My instincts tell me it's not that, though. I could see Finn and Ellen being ruthless enough – look how they ignored all our pleas to discuss the plans for our area – but would they knowingly get involved in something corrupt? It's not my impression of them."

Eve felt the same, but had to point out, "We don't know them all that well, Greta. And while I agree it seems unlikely, people do strange things where money is concerned."

"What about this Dr. Murray?" Niamh asked. "Eithne, could you see him bashing a person over the head?"

"I don't know," Eithne replied slowly. "I despise the man but I've never felt he was violent."

"He comes from a violent background, though. And maybe the feud between Gillespie and his father has continued into the next generation." Tom pointed out. "If not him, maybe someone close to him?"

"Tom, that actually makes sense!" Greta said, sounding unflatteringly surprised. Tom grinned at Eve.

"I have my moments." He said.

"That's a definite line of inquiry. Niamh, could you do some digging? You're on that genealogy site aren't you?"

Niamh nodded doubtfully. "It only has records up to the forties, Greta, they don't give out info on living people so handy."

"Use your initiative, woman. Ask one of your friends on there, and find out how to search for birth certificates and all that."

"Right." Niamh took out her phone and made a note. "First thing tomorrow."

Eve gave her mother a sympathetic glance. Greta would be hounding her by midday, looking for results. She was beginning to see how the podcast was so successful – Greta was relentless.

"I'll keep looking for some reason to halt the development," Eithne volunteered. "But while I'm on site, I'll chat to the workers. You never know – might be rumours or gossip that would put us on the right path."

"We need to talk to anyone who was there that night," Eve mused. "We sort of took for granted no one in the protest could be involved, and when that witness saw Boyd and his friends, it kind of distracted us. But really, we should have made it our business to interview everyone."

"Ronan will have a list," Greta said. "One of us should be on the picket line with each of them and just chat."

Everyone looked at Claudia, who sighed. Her talent for extracting information without anyone realizing they were spilling the beans exceeded even Niamh's. "I'll see what I can do, once I know their names. Tom, you were organizing the rota?"

"I still am, and I'll let you know when each is scheduled to take a turn."

Eithne clapped her hands. "This is a dream come through. I never thought I'd be in the heart of a Greta Goode investigation."

Dymphna snorted but refrained from comment. Greta preened but caught the look on Dymphna's face and refrained from crowing.

"Dymphna, you need to tackle Ellen again," Eve said. "Tell her we can't help her if they continue to keep secrets from us."

"Righto. Leave them to me."

Tom cleared his throat.

"If we're finished for the moment, Eve? I wanted to say – with everything going on we've really neglected to organize any holiday activities for the neighbourhood. I was talking to my brother today, and it occurred to me that one simple thing would be carolling. We could all get together some night, have a carol singing session out in the crescent, invite all the neighbours, everyone at the protest etc"

"That's a lovely idea," Eve felt a glow of affection for his thoughtfulness.

"We could serve some refreshments," Dymphna said. "Just tea and buns, that kind of thing. Hot chocolate, maybe."

"When though?" Eve calculated in her head. "Christmas Eve would be lovely but will everyone be busy?"

"We're talking about a few hours in the early evening," Dymphna said. "If they're busy, so be it, but if the rest of Bramble Lane are willing, I say we do it anyway."

There was a murmur of assent around the table.

"I'll be there!" Eithne Blennerville offered. "My wife and I have nothing planned for the twenty-fourth, and we were just saying we miss going to a carol service or a concert that night. And a few of my students are from abroad – usually Maeve and I host them over the break. Perhaps I could bring them along too? Some of them will never have experienced a traditional Irish Christmas before."

"The more the merrier!" The talk of carols and Christmas Eve ensured that it was a cheerful bunch who took their leave later that evening. The Professor seemed to have enjoyed herself mightily and left promising repeatedly to interrogate everyone she came across on the site, "Discreetly, I promise!"

All in all, a good day's work. Eve kissed Tom goodbye, glad he had returned earlier than expected from his family visit. Things were much easier to handle with him around, she admitted to herself. Even just knowing he was down the road was comforting.

When she had finished tidying up she looked out the kitchen window at the back garden fence. Luke from the Garden Centre was still busy, but had promised to make time for repairs as soon as possible. Eve had told him not to rush. What was the point in repairing a fence only to have it destroyed again a few days later? Until they knew what was going on out there, it might be as well to hold off on repairs.

She tried to feel the land beyond the garden boundary, but all she could sense now was silence, and a kind of watchfulness.

"Soon," she promised herself. "We'll figure out who killed Dolores and then I'm going to figure out what is going on out there."

She went to bed, tired but quite hopeful, to dream of funny

Christmas decorations, a plastic reindeer with a flashing red nose, two kids wandering around with bundles of hay and finally Dymphna Moriarty, fluttering around in the night sky, calling out "Merry Christmas, and a Happy New Year."

Chapter 19

Something woke Eve early the next morning, and despite her best efforts, she couldn't force herself to remain in bed. Giving up, reluctantly, she got up and showered, and was downstairs dressed and wide awake before the sky outside had lightened. On impulse, feeling there was something she'd overlooked about the day, she switched on the tv.

"It's the Solstice!" Eve stared at the television, watching the RTE news broadcast from the chamber at Newgrange. The programme cut from the studio to the ancient monument, and she watched as the sunlight entered the tunnel and travelled its length, until the burial chamber with its neolithic art was illuminated in wintry sunshine. An excited reporter informed the audience that it was the best display in five years, the day dawning bright and clear albeit bitterly cold along the Boyne.

"Well, that feels like a good omen!" Eve told herself. A renewed sense of purpose settled in her heart. Today, she wouldn't take no for an answer – everyone was going to finally give up their secrets and this mess would be cleared up. An early breakfast, a quick tidy up and she was ready to face the day.

She spied her neighbour from the living room window. From the set of Dymphna's shoulders and her determined stride, Eve guessed that she wasn't the only one in that frame of mind. She could hear Dymphna's imperious knock on the door of Holly Cottage from where she stood, followed by the unmistakable sound of an elderly woman on the warpath.

"Now, Ellen. I don't care how early it is."

Eve grinned. The Marrinans didn't stand a chance. She looked forward to hearing the full story from Dymphna later, but right now she had quite a lot to attend to herself.

Today was her last art class in the community centre, before the break. By common consent, the Christmas outing had been amalgamated with the plan to hold an afternoon carol service on Bramble Lane, but she still had some treats to bring in and a small present for each of the students. Before she did that, she needed to spend the morning productively – and she intended to start with young Ashleigh. School term ended that morning, and both kids would be home early so Eve decided to waylay them shortly after twelve. Which left her a few hours to do some digging and make some connections.

She sat at her computer, and opened the file marked Holly Cottage. In it she had lists and notes and half formed theories. Time to put it all together.

* * *

Finn Marrinan made the mistake of trying to stare down his neighbour. As a newcomer to the area, he could be forgiven for not realizing the futility of this action. To his credit, after a few minutes trapped in the beady, glittering depths of Dymphna dark eyes, he caved and tried a different approach.

"Mrs. Moriarty, please understand. We appreciate everything you and your friends are doing for Boyd, we truly do. But some things are private –"

"Don't be ridiculous." Dymphna lowered her bony frame into a chair and made herself comfortable. "In a murder investigation, nothing is private. And let me tell you, our Gardaí may move cautiously but they are thorough. They'll find out whatever it is you're hiding and then – precisely because you hid it – they'll consider it suspicious. Is that what you want?"

"Eh, no – of course not. But –"

"No ifs, buts or maybes, young man. Sit down, Ellen, for goodness sake. You're giving me the ick with your fidgeting. You too, Finn. Sit."

Not really sure why, both grown adults obeyed her and sat down meekly in their own living room. Ellen glanced at her husband and shrugged helplessly. Finn gave it one last try.

"I really must insist, Mrs. Moriarty –"

"Whisht. And call me Dymphna, will you? I think we're long past the formalities now, what with you trying to ruin the neighbourhood and us trying to save your son from a stint in Mountjoy prison."

Finn swallowed. "Well, Boyd has an alibi now."

"An alibi the Gardaí are more than half inclined to ignore. An alibi that relies on the word of two young people who also should not have been where they were, at that hour. What if they decide the three of them were involved?"

"Oh no!" Ellen shook her head, her dark curls bouncing. "They can't! What possible reason would those kids have to hurt Dolores?"

"What reason would Boyd have to hurt her?" Dymphna snapped. "You know why, don't you? And it starts with why you let Dolores McIntyre back into your lives."

She knew she had won when Ellen's face crumbled. "It'll make Boyd look bad, and it's not fair, it really isn't. He's such a good kid, and he was provoked."

"Ah." Dymphna gave a satisfied sigh and sat back in her chair. "Tell me all about it, pet. I reared a few kids myself, there's nothing I haven't seen or heard. I know how easy it is to give a kid a bad name."

Ellen seized on this eagerly. "That's it exactly. Because everyone was so angry with us, and blamed us for what Dolores did, they picked on Boyd and Melly. They lost everyone, even their best friends. Melly was bullied off the gymnastics team, but it didn't stop there. The kids in her year picked on her, mercilessly. They'd wait for her on the way home from school, take her money and her bags and throw her books into the mud – rotten, mean stuff."

"And Boyd got to hear about it?" Dymphna could see it all in her mind's eye – the big brother stepping in to help his kid sister, standing up to a bunch of bullies…but those bullies were younger than him…

"He gave a couple of them a box on the ear." Ellen said. "And someone caught it on video."

"Dolores." Finn said. "She saw it happening - or for all we know, she set it up. Whatever, she recorded it. Some of those brats, their parents wanted Boyd arrested for assault. But without evidence it was his word against theirs, and I – I made him lie. He was all for telling the cops exactly what happened but I was terrified. I was sure they'd make a huge deal of it."

"We moved here, partly to get away from it all. We thought a fresh start, and Boyd would be fine." Ellen let out a little sob, the mother at her breaking point with worry and regret.

"Then Dolores turned up, with the video and blackmailed you into making her a partner." Dymphna scowled. "She *was* a rotten cow, wasn't she?"

"It was all my fault," Finn said. "I couldn't let her ruin Boyd's fresh start, so I gave her what she wanted. And it seemed fine – she signed an agreement that limited her interference in the development. I figured, she'd get a pay out and be happy. In return she promised to destroy the recording of Boyd."

"And you believed her?" The disbelief in the older woman's voice made Finn wince.

"She deleted it in front of me, and swore there were no other copies. What could I do? And part of the contract she signed was a sort of non-disclosure agreement. If the video resurfaced, she'd get nothing out of the development. Not my finest hour, I know. But I was trying to do right by my boy."

"It was a fool's solution, from beginning to end. Did it occur to you that you just made a bigger mess by not letting Boyd be honest? No wonder the lad is angry with you."

Finn nodded. "I know. I know."

"Ach. No use crying into our beer over it, is there? But how much of this did Boyd know?"

"He didn't know about the recording, not until recently. He just thought – he thought we paired up again with Dolores to make money."

"And I dread to ask, but when did he find out about the video?" But Dymphna could guess the answer. She could recall the boy roaring at Dolores, his face red with anger.

Finn hesitated. "The day before the protest."

"Mother of divine!" Dymphna tapped her foot impatiently. "You should have told us. So, Boyd really did have a reason to be angry – a reason to kill, some might say. He must have worried that Dolores had copies, and was biding her time."

"No!" Finn exclaimed. "Dymphna, I know you don't know Boyd like we do but – first of all, he hated that we gave into her blackmail. He said we should have told her to do her worst, that he would happily explain that he was standing up for Melly. He said he should have done it back in Chicago, when he had the chance. He despised her, but he didn't care if she released it."

"And," Ellen added eagerly, "He would never hurt a woman. The kids back home – back in Chicago, I should say – they might have been younger but they were big, strong lads. Football players, big for their age. He never touched any of the smaller kids, or the girls at all. He just pulled the two big ones off of Melly and cuffed their ears…"

Dymphna closed her eyes. A lifetime of sensitivity to people, to stories, to words – she summoned it all to her aid. And she could hear the clear, loud ring of truth to the story. Not just the desperate need of parents to believe their child was incapable of true malice, but the cold and impartial sound of the truth.

"All right, calm down, I believe you," she said drily. "But you have made Boyd look twice as guilty as he already did. First things first – go to Detective Desmond and explain all of this. No – don't even try to argue, Finn. This is not a suggestion. If you don't, I will. Trust him. Now, what we need to figure out is this – what on earth was so important about this development that Dolores McIntyre would go to those lengths to get on board?"

* * *

Greta and Niamh had their work cut out for them, pouring over nearly a hundred emails and private messages from Goode Hunters. Most were just repeats of the kind of information Greta had already gathered – stories of how Dolores and her associates had ripped them off, or ruined their home town. But as they dug deeper one or two stood out.

"Look!" Niamh pointed to her laptop screen. "This is from a Leslie Carroll. Not sure if it's a man or a woman, isn't it funny how some names are unisex? Like Adrian. If you don't see it spelled out it could be Adrienne. I knew an Adrienne once, in school, awful pain she was."

"Niamh," there was an edge to Greta's voice. "What does the email say?"

"Oh. Sorry. Yes. Leslie says she or he knew Dolores back in the day, in college. Says she was a terrible person even then, and that she liked to hint about her gangland connections. Which Leslie says no one believed but that's funny too, cos we know now it was true. Liars, I suppose, you never know which bit is real and what's true."

Greta gritted her teeth. She knew Niamh had a mind like a steel trap, under all that waffle, and that anything her friend said could turn out to be vitally important, but dear heavens, there was an awful *lot* of waffle.

"Anything else?"

"Um…no, no…Oh!" Niamh looked up, her eyes sparkling. "This Leslie says, Dolores liked to swan around with her boyfriend…Declan Murray."

Greta had a smile like a shark in a swimming pool. "Well now. Email that Leslie person back and get the dirt."

* * *

Claudia wandered through the small group at the protest site. She had to admire the dedication,- despite the fact it was Christmas week and the work at the site was still halted, there had been a presence there every day. People seemed to be genuinely invested in it. And it seemed to have brought a lot of the community together. While Bramble Lane had always been a close-knit enclave, the long main road, and the newer estates built off it, were filled with busy families, working all day and keeping to themselves on weekends. But standing in the cold with a placard while a handful of security guards and construction workers glared at you seemed to have a bonding effect. People greeted each other by name, inquired after family members and shared plans for the coming festivities.

Claudia approved.

She saw the Professor hard at work in a corner of the field, and waved. One of the security guards turned to see what had caught her eye– the one who had been concerned for the protesters' safety on the first day, she recalled, the only one who seemed to mingle with the locals. And yet, for all his seeming friendliness, he struck her as sly.

Maybe his bosses had told him to gain their trust, keep an ear out for any hint of the protesters' plans. Two could play at that game.

"Good morning." Claudia gave her best smile, the one she used for greeting illustrious visitors to Brigade headquarters. "Cold morning, isn't it?"

The man edged closer. He had a short muscular body with a shiny bald head, and a graying goatee beard. He smiled but once again, Claudia thought – that smile doesn't reach his eyes, does it? But his tone when he spoke was warm and friendly.

"It's Baltic! But it's not raining, which is something. Don't mind the cold as long as it's not wet."

"You must be fed up, standing out here all day." Claudia pointed at the group of environmentalists, working their way through the field. "But of course, you can hardly leave that lot to their own devices."

His eyes narrowed, just a fraction. "Yeah. Bunch of toffee nosed students. And that Professor one – have you met her?"

"Only briefly. These academic types…" She let the sentence hang on the air, full of implications that the man could seize on if he wanted.

He did.

"That's the truth. You'd think she owned the place, telling us we can't step here or there. I mean, I've nothing against saving the environment, but telling my workers they can't do their job is where I draw the line."

"Ah. I suppose they're looking for plants and things? It must make your job difficult."

"You should know." There was no mistaking the sour note now, despite the grin remaining on his face. "Your lot called them in."

"Ah. Not my department, I'm afraid. It wouldn't have occurred to me." Claudia believed in sticking to the truth, even if it was stretched a little. She really wouldn't have thought of calling in the local university, but no need to tell the man she fully backed the decision.

"Oh. Sorry. Have you any idea how long they'll be here?" His tone was wheedling now.

"Not really, but I can't imagine they'll be much longer. They'll have to stop over the holidays, I presume."

He seemed to brighten up at this. "I suppose so. Anyway, I'd better get back to work."

"Nice chatting," Claudia murmured. Now, she wondered, why was he so put out by Eithne and her students? And why pretend to be friendly when underneath, he was anything but?

And why on earth did he look so familiar when she could swear she had never set eyes on him before. Maybe he sounded like someone...she smiled suddenly. A little piece of the puzzle had clicked into place.

* * *

Eithne Blennerville poked at a briar, pulling it back as far as possible to peer into the undergrowth. She needed to mark out the next section for her few remaining students. Most had headed home around the country for the holidays, and wouldn't return til the second week in January. Her overseas students had volunteered to keep searching, and they were making progress, but it was painfully slow.

Bending over, she noticed a rock that seemed out of place among the others. It was larger, and decorated with a series of spiral motifs. And it had "made in china" stamped in small letters on the side.

"What on earth?" Eithne pushed at the rock with her toe and it moved with a surprising ease.

Plastic! she thought. *One of those fake rocks you put in your garden and hid your keys under, although what genius decided to put a pretty design on it...talk about ruining the illusion.*

"It's a bit daft, isn't it?" A voice said behind her. She jumped, turning to see the familiar figure of the head security guard. He pointed at the plastic "rock" and repeated. "A bit daft. Some eejit thought it would be a good idea, why have an ugly rock in your garden, hiding the spare keys, when you could have a nice decorative one." He smiled coldly. "Of course, it made finding the keys very easy. After a few break=ins, no one would touch them. Still, they worked well enough while it lasted. We wrung our hands, apologized, and moved on. But I kept a few around, and a few years before he died, my dad gave one to his old pal, Patrick Gillespie."

Eithne tried to remain calm, and take in what the man was saying. Up til now, he'd just been a figure in the background. If anything, she'd have described him as a bit soft for a security guard, too willing to mix with the locals and generally nosey. The man confronting her now was anything but - his eyes were hard and empty, his tone lightly mocking.

"Your dad?" She tried to sound vaguely interested, and a little clueless. The last bit was easiest.

"Yes, my dad. Murray the Undertaker. You heard of him? You're not telling me you don't remember Dublin's greatest criminal?"

"I...I do recall the name. He was your dad? And Patrick Gillespie, he was a friend of his?"

"Gillespie was his rival. And I suppose, in a weird way, a mate. By the end, anyway. Dad sent him one of my plastic keyholder rocks as a kind of joke, I thought. But it was more than that. You see, Gillespie wanted to hide something, and my dad wanted to give me a shot at finding it too."

He grabbed Eithne's arm, as she made to move past him. "Oh no. No, Professor. Stay right where you are. Where was I? Ah. Yes. Gillespie told his niece where, but his description was vague. Only I knew exactly what it looked like. And Dolores being the impatient cow she always was, couldn't wait for it to turn up. She came to me, asking for help…But once I knew where to look I really didn't need her any longer."

He pointed at the rock. "Now, you might as well make yourself useful. Get digging."

"Do no such thing,"Claudia's authoritative tone made Liam Murray take a step backwards. Or it could have been the shock of finding two angry old women had crept up on them.

"You and Dolores were a well-matched pair," Dymphna said. "But you're not as smart as you think."

"Oh, I'm very smart." Liam produced a gun from the waistband of his jeans. "Did you think I wouldn't come prepared? Now, you pair stand over there. Professor, start digging, or one, or both, of these old biddies gets it."

Chapter 20

Eve had spent the morning combing through everything they had gathered so far and her head hurt with it all. Her earlier determination remained but the optimism was severely damaged. Dymphna had reported back to her, faithfully recounting the story as gleaned from the Marrinans. Now her neighbour was taking a turn on the picket line, while Eve was left to make sense of it all.

She had just turned to the notes Claudia had supplied, from her talk with Sahana Puri of the Irish Women's Brigade. Dolores, her mean-spirited attitude towards fellow cadets, her unsavoury family and the possibility of involvement, however tangentially, with Ireland's biggest security heist – all fascinating stuff but how to make it all fit? Claudia seemed sure it was relevant, which made Eve reluctant to dismiss any of it.

Just as she thought this, her phone pinged. Eve stared at a text from Claudia.

"On way to talk to Murray. Will report back later. Need to check something. Any word from Niamh - Murray's family?"

"Oh dear," she said out loud, "I hope she's careful." She realized she was talking to herself, and shook her head. "I'm turning into my mother."

"There are worst things you could do," Niamh remarked behind her, causing her daughter to scream and leap to her feet.

"Mam!"

"What? I let myself in, I didn't want to disturb you. You were hard at work."

Eve opened her mouth to point out that her mother couldn't possibly have known if she was working before choosing to let herself in unannounced -again. But it was pointless, partly because Niamh would produce some eye-watering example of her own peculiar logic which would be impossible to refute, but also make absolutely no sense at all. And partly because it was Niamh, and there was no way of knowing what she could and couldn't see, even through brick walls.

"You put the heart crosswise in me, you have to stop doing that."

"Ah gwon, you're fine. Do you want to hear my news? I got the full breakdown of the Murray family. There's a lot of them - some perfectly respectable and others, not so much. I've written it all out for you - there's a couple of siblings, and a shed-load of cousins. What are you up to anyway?"

"Looking through everything we have so far."

"How's it going?"

"I'm more confused now than I was," Eve admitted. "Dymphna called in earlier, she got the full story out of the Marrinans. Dolores had video of Boyd, that could have got him in trouble. Finn the eejit gave in and made her partner, on the condition that she destroyed the recording. But I'm not sure why she wanted to be partner in the first place. She didn't need the money and surely there were easier projects to get involved with. Oh, it's all there – I'm sure of it – I just can't see it."

Niamh tutted. "You've read it all? Don't you remember what I used to say to you before exams? Sit back now, let your mind wander. Do something repetitive – it's an awful pity you don't spin, Eve."

Eve blinked. Her mother aimed several reproaches at her over the years but not making her own yarn was a new one.

"It's perfect for this," Niamh elaborated. "If it was later in the day, we could light the fire and you could do a spot of fire-gazing.. But it's a waste when you're out all afternoon. I have it!" She clicked her fingers triumphantly. "When you were a kid you'd sit and doodle for hours. I knew you'd be an artist, even then. Sit down with some markers and paper and draw and let your mind rest. You'll see your connections then."

Before Eve could protest, she found herself sitting at the kitchen table, a blank sheet of white paper in front of her and a pile of markers her mother fetched from the small pantry Eve used to store art supplies. Niamh bustled about, making a pot of tea and rifling cupboards for biscuits, while giving a stream of consciousness lecture on the State of The World and What The Government Should Be Doing, all with the subtext of If Only Anyone Took The Time To Ask Me.

If she closed her eyes, Eve could imagine herself back in school, doing her homework while Mam made dinner. The sheer comfort and familiarity of it brought a lump to her throat. She winked away an errant tear and took up a marker. Thinking of childhood and school and days spent with her brother and mother, her hands moved of their own accord. Without realizing it, she covered a sheet, took another and continued her sketches.

At first she concentrated on the lines and marks on the paper but her brain soon let go, trusting to the muscle memory of hours of practise. Dolores McIntyre, her life in Dublin before the States, her close brushes with outright criminality, her blackmail of the Marrinans...Murray, with his gangland connections and the pair of them wandering around at night... looking for a rock with markings on it. Boyd and Ashleigh with young Sean, out at that hour of the night – armfuls of hay – and everything feeling so strange, so unseasonable. Sadness, and rows, and protests. As if something wasn't quite right with the world – her ear caught the tail end of Niamh's prattle.

"What? What did you say?"

Niamh looked up from her careful biscuit arranging. "I said these custard creams are as nice as the posh ones and half the price."

"No! Before that, Mam, about everything feeling wrong."

"Oh. That. Yes, I said that there's something off this year. Nothing feels right, there's no holiday spirit. It's the Solstice, and I don't know if you saw the broadcast but it was beautiful. Yet, here we are, embroiled in murder and trying to stop a last bit of greenery in the area being ruined and there just doesn't seem to be room for anything....*nice*."

Eve looked at her mother, then at the paper she had filled with drawings. The first sheet was simple to explain, her brother's smiling face and scenes of family life. The second – there was Dolores, sneering out at her. In the background a Hawk and a Coffin – and a pile of money. Boyd and his hoodie, scowling. A group scene with little figures and placards and security men.

But these were all tiny sketches around one large central one.

"Armfuls of bloody hay!" Eve sprang to her feet, then hesitated. It was urgent, vital even, but the murder came first.

"Mam, listen to me. I know what's been going on, what damaged my fence and why the kids were out in the field that night. I know. And it's – it's terribly important. But we need to clear up the murder first, and then we can fix everything. Okay? Say okay, Mam. Good. Now, don't ask questions, don't argue. Just…put as much protection and energy into that field as you can, understand? Get Dymphna to help you. Get everyone who isn't busy. Even Tom – just tell him it's a meditation session or something, I don't care."

Niamh gave her a long, appraising look, then nodded. "Will do. Look forward to the explanation."

Eve glanced at the sheet of paper, still clutched in her hand and thrust it at her mother.

"There's your explanation."

Niamh looked at it, her mouth open.

"Oh."

* * *

"Do have some more," Claudia pushed another bun towards Dr. Murray. "It's nice to see someone appreciate my baking."

Murray hesitated, but only for a moment. "Well, now, I suppose it is almost Christmas, eh?" He took a huge bite of one of Claudia's Christmas cake muffins, each individually iced, mini fruit cakes, liberally fed with whiskey. And other special ingredients, not least of which was her iron will and intent.

"You must tell me," she purred encouragingly, "How did you get involved with the development? I suppose a man of your reputation and stature must get asked to do lots of consulting work?"

Claudia had charmed the environmentalist lecturer into a meeting, by hinting at a lucrative series of talks with the various Brigade branches nationwide. Murray had hummed and hawed, saying it was end of term and he was only in his office tidying up some administrative issues, but the mention of a very generous fee had changed his mind. Now they were both seated in the Staff canteen of the Leinster University Arts building, drinking rather bad coffee and eating excellent cakes. Murray needed little encouragement to talk about himself, a carefully curated version that showed him at his best. Claudia was content to wait until the cake did its job before tackling the tougher questions.

"I am in demand, if I may say so myself. You see, so many of my colleagues are well-meaning but totally unrealistic. We can't afford to protest over every little patch of ground, not in this economic climate. Now, the bigger environmental picture – that's where my interests lie. We need to get big business on board, Mrs. Warren, and we won't do that by opposing them at every turn. No, what's needed is a more diplomatic approach and that's my policy. Unless there is a clear and urgent reason to deny permission to building or development, I believe we should work with the system…"

Every question prompted a long winded answer, to which Claudia only half listened. Like Murray, she too was interested in the big picture. That the man was self-serving, she had no doubt. But was he corrupt or foolish? Or both? She suspended her conscious thoughts, those voices that filtered things through their own bias, and opened up her unconscious. And she listened.

"I probably shouldn't tell you this…" Murray giggled, leaning forward conspiratorially, "But I knew poor Dolores, the woman who was killed on the Bramble Lane site. I knew her quite well, back in the day."

"Oh! How exciting, Doctor. And how sad for you, that must have been very upsetting." Claudia suppressed a smile, judging that her cake recipe was well on the way to helping loosen Murray's tongue.

"Sad? Um, a bit I suppose. If I'm honest, couldn't stand the woman. We used to date, in our University days. She was very exciting, Claudia, very passionate. I was quite smitten. But she was also – mean. And arrogant. She once told me I was "second rate," can you imagine that? Second rate. She was going to be a big shot, that was her plan. Obsessed with money, and not above a bit of dodgy dealing, if you get my meaning. No, by the end, I was well shot of her."

Claudia looked at him with interest. "Yet, you agreed to work with her on this project?"

"Oh that. Well, water under the bridge and all that. Besides, she was paying well. And her partners were respectable enough. I would have refused otherwise, no matter what Liam said."

"Liam?"

"My brother. He asked me to get involved, as a favour. Said they needed a sensible, reliable environmentalist on their side. "

Claudia practically held her breath.

"He's a partner then? In the development?"

"Yeah. No. Sort of, ha ha. His firm has the contract for security for the site, so you see it was important to him that it went ahead."

"Head of security?" Claudia closed her eyes and whistled through her teeth. "Your brother, Liam Murray, is a security guard on the site."

"He's the boss, not a mere guard." Murray said, offended. "He owns a huge and very successful security company. Which, hee hee, is rather funny – when you consider what our dad did for a living." He roared laughing, full of good humour at his own joke.

Claudia gave him a look that would have sent any of her junior brigade members scrambling for cover. Murray was far too pleased with himself to notice,

"I think I've met him," she said. "About your height, bald, goatee beard…"

"That's him! Gas man, Liam. He was a bit wild in his youth, didn't go the same route as me. To be honest, he followed in Dad's footsteps there for a while, but sure, that was hardly surprising. When Dad retired, he went straight – set up the security firm."

"And has been very successful." Claudia made a mental note to tell Detectives Desmond and Cullen to check every job Liam Murray's firm had been on and cross check with break-ins, robberies and so forth.

"I have to get back now, Dr. Murray. Thank you so much for your time, and we'll be in touch with you in the New Year, I'm sure. " Claudia gathered up the remains of her buns and stood. "You've been most helpful."

"Of course, of course. Lovely to meet you. And if you see Liam again –"

"Oh," Claudia's smile was grim. "I'm sure I will."

* * *

Claudia's second text arrived just as Eve pulled the door to Kimberly Cottage shut behind her.

"Murray's brother Liam. Security on site. On way there now to tell Dymphna. Come meet."

Like a kaleidoscope the pieces of information floating around Eve's head turned, twisted and slotted into place. Before she had left Kimberly Cottage, she had read Niamh's rough Murray family tree. It seemed they had both reached the same conclusion, from different points. She could only hope Claudia and Dymphna would wait for her to arrive before confronting the older Murray brother.

She considered this for a moment, thought about the two women, and realized that was highly unlikely. She paused only to ring Ronan Desmond's mobile, giving an exasperated moan as it went to voicemail. She tried his partner, Cullen, but the same thing – no answer, only a curt "Detective Cullen's phone, please leave a message."

"Cullen, you and Ronan need to get here. I know who killed Dolores McIntyre, and so does Claudia. And the mad old bint has gone to the site to confront him." She added the bare details, and hung up – she couldn't wait for the Gardaí, not while the others might be in danger.

Eve glanced at her watch as she half-walked, half-jogged to the protest at the site's main entrance. She should have been on her way to Art class, instead of hurrying to confront a murderer. The afternoon was getting darker by the moment, the morning sunshine giving way to heavy grey clouds. It was dark even for a December afternoon in Dublin, and many of the cars on the main road had full headlights on. A few passers-by glanced at her curiously as she hurried past, but she ignored them. Well aware that she had a woollen hat jammed askew on her head and not a screed of makeup on her face, she didn't care. Something told her to get to Dymphna and the field as soon as she could.

There were three other local residents at the gate, all carrying placards, but no sign of Dymphna.

"She was here," one woman said, looking around. "I was talking to her. Then a friend of hers arrived…"

"They went over there –"A man pointed to the far side of the site, the back of Bramble Lane. "They were talking to one of the security guards."

Eve looked around. In the distance, at the end that backed onto Bramble Lane, she could just make out a small group of figures. She squinted, but could only be reasonably sure that the black clad figure was Dymphna. The university students were at the far end of the field, their backs to the action. She couldn't see the Professor.

"Are you all right, missus?" A small boy tugged on her sleeve. She looked into the anxious face of Ciarán Phelan, and forced a smile.

"I'm just a bit worried about my friends, pet. But I think I see them down there."

"Are they in trouble?"

"I hope not. But here, where's your mam?"

Mags called out, "Is he bothering you? Ciarán, stop bothering the lady."

"He's fine, honestly. But look – the Gardaí are on their way." Or at least, she fervently hoped they were. "Please, when they arrive, send them down to that group over there, see the lady in black?"

"Sure." The woman frowned. "Here, what's going on."

"No time," Eve replied, "Just, send the Gardaí over to us as soon as they get here."

She set off at a run, not bothering to worry about the uneven ground and treacherous rabbit holes this time. It was a long time since Eve had run for anything more challenging than a bus, and it showed. Added to her lack of cardio fitness was the fact that the green space seemed to expand, as she ran. It felt as if she would never reach them, as if she was in one of those nightmares where the things you needed were just out of reach – and then suddenly she was nearly there and the group became clearer despite the wintry gloom.

Claudia, in her green wax jacket standing stiff and straight as ever, Dymphna in her customary black skirts and top with a heavy fleece, also in black– and kneeling down, almost hidden from view was Professor Eithne Blennerville. Looming over her, one eye keeping watch over the other ladies, was the man she had come to think of as Smarmy Security Guard. Declan Murray's brother.

"Keep digging or one of these old bats gets it!" The man's voice – Eve recognized it immediately. It was so similar to his brother's she had assumed the environmentalist was the man they had heard out with Dolores that night. He was a similar height, and build too. A goatee beard, bald head, short and broad…they could have been twins.

And, Eve realized, by some miracle -considering she was gasping for breath and her heart was hammering so loudly in her chest she felt sure it was audible to everyone – he hadn't yet noticed that she was there.

She froze in place, trying to breath quietly. Dymphna caught her eye and gave an almost imperceptible nod, with a small incline of her head. Eve followed the hint, and saw a spade, lying on its side, abandoned beside Liam Murray. If she bent down, really quietly and quickly, could she reach it in time to whack the man over the head? She doubted it. The last few minutes had robbed her of any illusions as to her speed and agility. She gave Dymphna a desperate shake of the head and her neighbour rolled her eyes. Claudia shifted slightly, drawing Murray's attention and ire to herself.

"Stand still, or I'll make you," he snarled. On the ground, Eithne took the opportunity to grab a decent sized rock, from the pile of earth and stones she had disturbed with her digging. She brought it down hard on Murray's foot and was rewarded by a scream of pain and a string of curses.

"You stupid –" Liam raised his hand and to Eve's horror, it became clear why the women had been obeying his commands. A small black gun – a sight unseen and unheard of in most Irish people's lives, an object seen only in movies, in newsreels of the Rising and subsequent War of Independence, and on news reports about other places, other people's experiences. Eve had only ever seen a shotgun once, held by a farmer out shooting pests on his own land. A gun! In this special place, this green land, at this special time of year –

Horror gave way to absolute rage. This bully of a man terrorizing her neighbours had to be stopped. Without any conscious decision, Eve did two important things, at the same time. The first was a silent wail of righteous indignation, a call to the very land itself *and all that found shelter on it*. The second was a smooth, lightning fast move to the left, which caused Murray to spin in her direction and away from the others. As she moved, his arm raised, the gun pointed directly at her and – a bloodcurdling, bone chilling scream of terror came from the man, as he stepped backwards, staring at something over Eve's shoulder.

She stepped out of the way, and turned to look. And there it was, magnificent and terrible and glorious, and utterly impossible. Antlers that filled the sky, large brown eyes that pierced the soul, smooth brown flanks and a thick, strong neck. A noble head, and hooves that pawed at the frozen ground leaving deep gouges as if it was soft mud. An aura of power, and magic, and hope and all the things that make us get up every morning, even in the dark times.

And it was angry. Like the land was angry. Like Eve was angry. It lowered its huge head, fixed Murray with a glowering stare and prepared to charge. Their erstwhile captor responded with a moan of abject fear and curled up into a ball on the ground.

"Keep it away from me!" he gibbered.

Claudia bent over him, snatching the gun from his trembling hand and snapped, "Three times All Ireland Shooting champion, Sonny Boy. Twitch, and you lose a part of yourself you value."

Eve couldn't take her eyes from the apparition in front of her. She raised a hand, trembling a little herself, and reached out tentatively. She stroked the creatures neck and murmured, "It's all right, it's all right. Thank you, thank you so much."

The head swung in her direction, the antlers causing her to duck, but the eyes that met hers were soft now, and full of kindness. She ran a hand over the beast, looking for signs of injury and there it was – a nasty cut along his left leg, healing now but obviously deep and painful when received.

"Ashleigh and Sean," She whispered. Those liquid eyes met hers again and she nodded. "Of course. And Boyd Marrinan too. They risked everything rather than betray you, you know that? Yes. So what are we going to do about you?"

"We're going to hide him," Dymphna said, " and quickly. Look!"

Running across towards them was Ronan Desmond and his partner, with an entourage of uniformed Gardaí, students armed with trowels and shovels and the protesters – including wee Ciarán and his mother Mags. Ciarán was howling possibly the weirdest battle cry in Irish history - "Leave the Art Lady Alone!"

By the time Eve glanced back at her friends, Dymphna was nowhere to be seen, but the reindeer – such a mundane word, for the strange and beautiful creature, Eve thought – was following a small fluttering object, deep into the trees and bushes.

"Don't worry," Claudia grinned. "I doubt they could see him anyway. Only the young, the very young at heart, and people like us."

"He saw it," Eve pointed at the unfortunate man, still moaning to himself on the ground.

"Only because she let him."

"She?" Eve blinked. "The reindeer is a she?"

"Of course. Only females have antlers in Winter, girl. "

Chapter 21

Detective Cullen hauled the erstwhile security guard into the back of the squad car, while Ronan took a quick statement from the ladies.

"You can give a full account tomorrow," he said. "Go home and get some rest, all of you."

They didn't need to be told twice. Eithne helped Eve escort Claudia over the rough ground back to the main road, where Sergeant Jo Maguire was waiting to give them all a lift back to Bramble Lane.

"We'll have to secure the scene over night," she remarked to Eve. "At least it's not a murder this time."

Within an hour, Eve's kitchen was once again filled with friends and neighbours, her mother having rounded up Tom and Greta, following Eve's instructions to send as much protection and good energy towards the green space as possible. They were all owed an explanation, she knew, but first –

"I need a cup of tea and something nice to eat," Eve demanded. "And I'm going to sit in an armchair and someone is going to bring it to me. Claudia, Eithne, you too. And when Dymphna gets in, she can sit with us. Then, and only then, will you get a word out of me."

Dymphna wasn't long behind them. She nodded approvingly as a cup of steaming tea and a plate of biscuits appeared in front of her. She stretched her legs out and sighed. "I need new glasses. I almost hit the satellite dish on the side of Tom's house."

She cocked an eye at Eithne and added, "I meant, the side wall. Of his house. Obviously. Not the satellite dish, which would be ridiculous."

Eithne smiled. "You'd have to be flying, to hit that. So yeah. Let's just say the side wall."

Dymphna winked at the Professor. "You're a good girl. Are you related to Moira Blennerville, by any chance."

"My aunt."

"Ah. That explains it, so."

Tom sat on the arm of Eve's chair. "Well, are ye ready to fill us in yet? I confess, I'm bewildered. All Jo Maguire would tell me is that the murderer has been caught, and you lot had a hand in it."

Eve looked at Claudia. "You want to start?"

"No, you tell it. I'll correct you if you go wrong."

"Right, then. I'm not one hundred percent sure about all of it, but I'll stake money I'm right when I say, all of this started back in the nineties. Both Dolores and the Murray brothers come from gangland families. Dolores' mother moved away to get out of that life, and she gave her daughter every advantage – but something in Dolores was drawn to the crooked side of the family. She studied in Dublin, joined the Brigade and got in with her uncle Patrick Gillespie. The Hawk. Declan Murray, he moved into academia and while I wouldn't say he's the most honest man in Ireland, he's not an out and out gangster. Unlike his brother, Liam."

"Liam created his security firm, his supposedly legitimate business, to cover up his criminal activities. I can't wait to see what Ronan turns up, once they start looking at it closely. But there was one thing from the past that haunted both Dolores and Liam. The Safe Hands Ireland heist. Dolores had a small but pivotal role in that, you see. Claudia figured it out, with the information she got from Sahana Puri. Dolores knew that the priceless Malachy Quinn coin collection was being moved, prior to auction. That poor man was determined to leave a legacy behind, to help others – and she decided to help herself to it."

"She was a rotten person," Greta interjected, "She left some trail of destruction behind her."

Eve nodded. "She did. This was particularly horrible though. She betrayed the Brigade, as well as thwarting a dying man's wishes. It set the tone for everything she did afterwards. But it backfired on her – The Hawk was happy to let her supply information about the robbery but he had no intention of sharing the spoils to that degree. Not with an upstart niece he barely knew. How it went down, no one may ever know but I'd say it was something like this – to keep her in line, to make sure she didn't double cross him like she did everyone else, he hid the coins. And probably some proof of her involvement – something she wrote, perhaps, giving details of when the collection would be moved. Dolores emigrated to the United States, her uncle retired from "business," and the Criminal Assets Bureau destroyed the organization built up by his rival, the Undertaker. Liam Murray continued in a more low-key way, hiding behind his bogus security firm."

"So how did she find out the location of the coins?"

"Gillespie died. In fairness, she had kept her mouth shut

all these years so he divulged the information to her, after his death. Ellen said it – she said Dolores returned home to Ireland because of a bereavement. And that it was Dolores who had mentioned Bramble Lane and the possibility of developing the land in the first place. She must have been furious that Finn got there first. But she had an ace to play – the recording of Boyd dealing with those thugs who bullied Melly."

"So that's how it went. Finn cut her in on the deal. Dolores hooked up with Liam – she knew him well, from the old days, when she dated Declan Murray. They used the development to search for the coins, but Murray didn't see any reason why he should share with her. And I'll bet she was trying to blackmail him too – she really couldn't be trusted, even by her fellow crooks."

"He must have thought all his Christmases had come at once, when poor Boyd was blamed!" Dymphna said.

"He would have let the kid swing," Tom said. "Disgusting man."

Eve agreed. "They were two horrible, rotten people."

"All this leaves one issue outstanding, though." Greta leaned forward, her eyes sparkling. "The Quinn Collection – it's still out there."

Eve blinked. "And it can stay out there, one more night won't make any difference. If you think I'm going out again, into that flipping field, to dig up buried treasure with you..."

"I never suggested such a thing." Greta sat back, her face a picture of innocence. "But sure, now you mention it..."

* * *

"The Quinn Coin Collection," Eve couldn't help a little glow of triumph as she handed the heavy, plastic container over to Ronan. The detective stared at her, then at the box, then back at her.

"Yiz went back out, didn't ye?" His west of Ireland accent reasserted itself in moments of stress or disbelief. "For the love of – Do none of ye do as you're asked?"

"It was Greta," Eve shrugged. "Before I knew what she was about, she had us up and digging. Look, I'm sure you would have preferred forensics and a team of careful excavators, but you have to admit this cuts through a lot of red tape. And paperwork. Eithne Blennerville had it half out of the ground anyway."

The detective closed his eyes.

"Grand so. I'll just alter my report, and Cullen's, then. Shall I say we found the coins, or will I name you? Or Greta?"

Eve knew he would be all right, once he had time to calm down. She plied him with cake and tea until the talk turned to Margaret and the young man's face lit up.

"I have a plan," he said proudly. "I'm going to propose on Christmas Eve, at the carol singing."

Eve raised an eyebrow. A public proposal was her idea of hell, but everyone was different.

"Have you – has she ever mentioned how she'd like to be proposed to?"

"You're worried about it being in front of everyone?" Ronan laughed. "No worries, I've sounded her out and to be honest, I doubt it'll come as a surprise. But she's had so little fun in recent years, since her parents died and she's been all alone, she would love a little fuss. And with everyone there to congratulate her, especially you and the auld ladies, it won't be as obvious that her own folk aren't around to see it."

Eve looked at him, a lump in her throat. "Ronan, if she doesn't grab you with both arms she's an absolute fool."

The young man went bright red and cleared his throat. "Not at all, sure I'm lucky to have her."

At least, that's one nice thing this year, Eve thought after the detective had left. "Maybe things are looking up." They still had a major problem, in the form of a large, antlered, magical creature wandering the field. Ashleigh had almost cried in relief when the ladies had tackled her, equally glad that the secret was now shared and that they didn't consider her certifiable.

There was also the small issue of what a magical reindeer implied. Like most adults Eve was absolutely clear on who and what Santa was. And yet – it was hard to deny the existence of a giant antlered creature that could appear and disappear, especially less than a week before Christmas Eve. When she broached the subject with the teenagers, Ashleigh stared at her with the pity usually reserved for unfortunates in their dotage.

"Who else could it belong to?" she asked.

"I don't know," Eve admitted, "but there could be other explanations. It could be from another dimension, or be from the sacred isles of Irish mythology or be a normal reindeer that somehow got enchanted."

"Look, in my experience," said the world-wise sixteen year old, "If it quacks like a duck, and waddles, and likes to swim in ponds, and tastes good with Cantonese sauce, it's almost certainly a duck. My dad had a saying – if you hear hooves, in Ireland, think horses not zebras. This is a horse, Ms. Caulton, not a zebra."

Boyd was a little less sure. "I'm not saying it is or it isn't." His American no nonsense upbringing showed itself. "But –

whatever it is, it's special. It's everything, just to know it exists. All we need to do now is figure out how to help it."

And that, thought Eve, was indeed the problem.

"Why did it keep kicking my fence down?" she mused, over coffee with the elder ladies.

"What were you doing when it happened?" Niamh asked.

"Nothing much. Well, it started when I put up decorations. I was thinking about my first real Christmas in Kimberly Cottage, about the plans I had for December." Eve paused and thought hard. "Actually, the next time was just after Tom and you put up extra decorations to cheer me up. And then again, after I got home from shopping in town – I was thinking how lovely the city centre was, the lights were magnificent, there was such a great atmosphere…"

The five women exchanged a look.

"It's drawn to a surge in goodwill." Dymphna helped herself to another chocolate biscuit and a fresh pour of tea. "It must feed off it. It was trying to get closer to you, because it recognized the energy."

Eve slapped the table with the palm of her hand. "Of course! And have you noticed? There was such a bad, down feeling around us all for the last few weeks? It must have been unable to heal because of it, because of the lack of joy and indeed, any goodwill."

"The solstice gave it a burst of energy," Greta remarked. "But now it needs a full blast, so it can get back to where it needs to be."

Eve sat back and grinned. "I know exactly what we need to do – and it starts now. Operation Goodwill and Joy, Ladies, commencing now."

* * *

Professor Eithne Blennerville straightened up and rubbed her aching back. Her last few students had chosen to stay late with her and work on the field, hoping against hope to turn up one single thing that might persuade either Finn Marrinan or the council not to go through with the development. Hope however, was fading as quickly as the winter's day. As the afternoon darkened, she had directed their attentions towards the thickest clump of trees and undergrowth, at the back of Bramble Lane. She cast a longing glance at Eve's battered fence, and thought of everything that had happened since she had volunteered to help the protest.

"What wouldn't I give to be in there with a cup of tea," she thought. "Ah well, onwards and upwards." Aloud, she said to her students, "You've all done so well, I'm awfully proud of you. We'll give it a few more minutes and then I think we'll have to call it a day."

No point in telling them it was unlikely they'd be back after the Christmas break, they had poured heart and soul into this. Let them enjoy the holidays…

A flutter just above her head made Eithne stand upright and gasp. A bat! But no ordinary one. In fact, not like any other species native to Ireland, she'd bet her year's salary on it. Around her, the young people stood stock still, watching the little winged creature.

"Professor!" One of them said, his voice quivering with excitement, "It's – it's not a Common and it's not a Leisler's."

A short girl, with thick curly hair and tortoiseshell rimmed glasses crept forward, her phone screen open on a page with images of the nine species known in Ireland.

"Professor," she breathed. "It's not like any of them."

Eithne grabbed the phone from the girl's hand and opened the camera app, snapping pictures like the world depended on it.

"Ladies and Gentlemen," she said, "I think we found our miracle."

Chapter 22

Later that evening Eithne Blennerville got her wish, seated in front of Eve's fireplace and giving an excited account of their discovery.

"It's a rare, almost unprecedented species. There's only one other possible sighting and that was in Morroco, in the nineties."

The other ladies turned to look at Dymphna, who looked smug.

"I've been to Morroco," she said. "Had a lovely holiday there in the nineties, funny enough."

Eithne ignored the interruption. "It's almost guaranteed to mean the work will stop. That entire area has to be preserved now. A rare bat species, making its habitat in our city – oh, it'd give you hope for the world, so it would!"

Greta gave an evil little chuckle as something occurred to her. "So, who's going to break the news to Finn and Ellen then?"

Eve felt a tiny stab of guilt. She could only hope the Marrinans wouldn't lose too much money if the development was shelved, but preserving the green space had to come first. The old women are rubbing off on me, she thought. I don't think I used to be this ruthless…

Dymphna volunteered to tell Finn and Ellen. It felt only fair, she said. She was expecting disappointment, dismay and possibly even rage. Instead –

"That's amazing!" Ellen looked at her husband and they exchanged a smile.

"Dymphna, we had already decided to scrap the building project."

"Really? But – why? I thought you had all your money tied up in this scheme."

"We had some, yes." Finn grabbed Ellen's hand. "But it almost cost us our family. Not just Boyd being charged, but him hating us and Melly thinking we were greedy and uncaring…"

"It wasn't worth it," Ellen said. "And besides, we still have plans for the land."

"It's time this community got what it needs. And deserves. I plan on offering a solution to the council – we'll build a playground, and may some kind of skate park for teens, and maintain the land, on their dime. And we'll sign over the land to them, as long as it's used only for the community. And to keep those bats safe."

Dymphna experienced something she rarely encountered. Utter surprise.

And a little chagrin that she had spent an hour trying to get Eithne's attention, fluttering around like a demented…but still, all's well in the end, she chided herself.

"Finn, Ellen, I can safely say that's the best Christmas present you could give us. People will be delighted. And if I might suggest something…you could announce it tomorrow at the street party."

Ellen clapped her hands. "Yes! And we can finally get to meet the neighbours properly – not over a protest line."

* * *

Christmas Eve dawned, and turned out to be one of those rare, perfect Winter days that Ireland occasionally experiences. A pale sunlight turned the sky baby pinks and blues, with creamy white clouds streaked across the horizon, while the air was crisp and clear.

Eve had marshalled the troops, from Jenny Chan and her friends to the local residents committee that had helped organize the protest. The weather forecast promised that there would be no rain on December 24th, and even the most pessimistic among them conceded that the outdoor celebrations could go ahead.

"Spread the word," she told them. "Three o'clock, tomorrow afternoon, everyone come to the main gate. We're going to hold the party on the land, to celebrate some great news. Everyone is invited and I know it'll be Christmas Eve, but *please* do come. There'll be food and refreshments – and if anyone wants to contribute, drop stuff up to the field before three. There's going to be face painting, and a juggler and all kinds of things. And then a big carol singing session – all your favourites."

Her enthusiasm did the trick, and the following afternoon saw a steady trickle of volunteers armed with home baked goods, flasks and large kettles for tea and coffee, portable plastic tables unearthed from sheds and in one notable case, a giant inflatable plastic pink flamingo wearing a Santa hat.

"For decoration," the owner Alyx explained. "Where will I stick it?"

"Anywhere you like," Claudia said. "But make sure it's

somewhere people can see it." If anything could cheer people up, it would be a pink flamingo.

Eve took charge of the face-painting and other crafty bits, with her art class. Claudia and her Irish Women's Brigade whipped the rest into shape, displaying the kind of efficiency that had toppled an Empire a century previously. The rest of the older ladies divided their time between making the refreshment displays attractive and chatting to anyone they could.

Eve caught snippets as she worked, rippling through the crowd.

"Time to celebrate…put the unhappy events behind us… special day, especially for the kiddies…"

"So nice to be part of something, especially these days. We really do have lovely neighbours, don't we?"

"You know, when you think about it she's right – it's not important if we have lots of presents and a perfect turkey. This is what it's all about. Look at wee Ciarán, he's having a ball…"

Like a stone dropped into a calm lake, the effects spreading out in ever-widening circles. Eve bent over the children who present smiling, trusting faces and asked, "Tiger, Fox or Unicorn?"

"Batman?" one asked hopefully and Eve shrugged.

"Sure, why not?"

"Thanks, missus. This is brilliant, isn't it? Will we be doing this every year?"

"You know what? I bet we will."

Claudia sought her out, introducing an elderly woman with the words, "This is Eimear Quinn. Her husband was Malachy Quinn, the coin collector."

Eve shook hands with Eimear, who thanked her for finding

the long lost collection.

"It was Malachy's pride and joy," she said. "It was a terrible blow for him when it was stolen. He was heartbroken, it was - it was his legacy. He wanted it to be sold, to raise money for charity."

"I'm so sorry. Dolores and her family really had a lot to answer for."

"They did. But sure, the poor woman paid a heavy price in the end. At least, I have the collection back and I can finish what my husband started. The collection will go from the Gardaí to an auction house, and they estimate it's worth ten times what it would have fetched in the nineties. So that's a bonus, isn't it?"

"That's wonderful. Where will you donate the proceeds?"

"I've decided to give half of it to the Children's Hospital as Malachy had wanted. And I'm dividing the rest among a few causes - refugees, the local community centre, and the women's shelter."

"I like it!" Claudia said approvingly. "Spread the joy."
"The community centre will be delighted, I know. I teach art there, and we need to provide more classes. This is a huge help."
If the party hadn't already cheered people up, the news of the Quinn Collection windfall did the trick. It looked as if the Parent and Kids painting class would become a reality in the new year, as well as other classes. And no one could begrudge the other charities their good luck, the world needing all the good deeds it could get.

Tom wandered by several times, bringing a succession of cups of tea, biscuits, and snippets of news. During a lull in the demand for face painting, he hovered around, looking anxious.

"Tom, either there's something on your mind, or you want

me to paint your face -which is it?"

"It's not face painting." Tom looked at his feet. "Eve, I wanted to ask you something. I know it's only been a few months but we have talked a lot about …us. About where we see this going. I wanted to say - you're a great friend. I really value that. But the way I feel about you is much more than friendship. I would like to be able to call you my girlfriend. I know we're a bit long in the tooth for boyfriend, girlfriend. My partner, if you prefer. But I want us to be an official couple." He produced a clumsily wrapped present, and thrust it at her.

She opened it, to reveal an ornate, gilded carriage clock.

"I don't have much to offer, Eve, but my time. Whatever time we both have left, I'd like to think we could spend it together."

Eve was glad it was hard to see clearly in the late afternoon, because she was fairly sure her cheeks were bright red. A bubble of nervous laughter threatened to come out. It was laugh or cry, her heart brimming over. She giggled, blushed even more furiously and then managed to say, "I'd like that. I mean, I feel the same way about you, and to me, we already are - but, it would be nice to be official. And I adore the clock. I'd like to spend my time with you, too."

Tom grabbed her hand and squeezed, beaming. "Lovely. Lovely. So, with your kids coming tonight you'll be busy but how about we tell them over Christmas dinner?"

Eve had a mental image of Mairead looking sternly at Tom and demanding to know his intentions, and had to choke down another bout of giggles. "Perfect." They stood looking at each other in a way that any pair of teenager lovers would had called "cringey" until a fresh wave of small children demanded to be transformed into fierce or magical creatures. Tom made himself scarce, only to be replaced by a pale-faced, stressed looking Ronan Dempsey.

"How's it going?" He didn't want for Eve to answer. "I can't find Margaret anywhere. Have you seen her?"

Eve eyed him shrewdly. "She'll be with the choir. Isn't she the main soloist?"

A motley crew of locals with singing experience and some pretense at being able to carry a tune had been gathered, under the unlikely leadership of Detective Cullen. Ronan had let slip that his partner had sung in the Garda choir for years, and Dymphna had overheard. Cullen had been volunteered before he could protest, but he had risen manfully to the occasion. He had a great ear, and soon sorted out the various singers. He had even persuaded young Ciara Bailey to sing, much to the delight of her friends. Jenny and the others were delighted to see her step into the limelight for once.

"Oh. Yes. of course." Ronan rubbed a hand over his face. "I forgot." One hand slipped into his coat pocket, and immediately out again. Eve shook her head.

"Ronan, if you'll take some unsolicited advice, wait until after the choir sings."

The young detective blinked. "What?"

She nodded at his coat pocket. "Don't do it in a rush. Wait until she has sung and then take her to one side, and do it properly."

He looked at her, then nodded in return. "Yeah. Yeah, that makes sense. Eve, do you think - do you think she'll be pleased?"

"Ronan, I think she'll be delighted. Now relax, and wait for the right moment."

By the time it was fully dark, at five o'clock, the impromptu choir had gathered in a large semi circle facing the line of tables and the expectant crowd. Detective Cullen stepped up front and cleared his throat.

"Before we start, Finn and Ellen Marrinan would like to say a few words…" Cullen announced.

The couple stepped forward, looking a little shy and nervous.

"I think," Finn said, "We can safely say that Ellen and I didn't get off to the best start here in Dublin."

A laugh from the crowd broke the tension and someone called out, "That's an understatement!"

"Okay, we got off to a pretty horrendous start. And there have been misunderstandings on both sides -"

"Mainly your side," Dymphna said loudly.

"-Mainly my side. Okay, you don't need to rub it in. But hey, despite it all, when we needed help, you guys looked after us. We'll never forget that."

He looked at Dymphna and the other senior ladies, and nodded. "We will always be in your debt."

Ellen took over. "We made a mistake, thinking that a big housing development was what this area needed. But it's time now to put it all right, and with that in mind, Finn and I are delighted to announce that this space will become the Merrion Community Park. There'll be a playground, a skateboard area, a garden and of course, we'll be preserving the habitat of the rare bat species…I don't know if it has a name, even?…still, we'll make sure it's safe."

The locals made their feelings known with a huge shout of approval and the Marrinans were surrounded by well-wishers, thanking them for the good news

Cullen waited til the noise had settled down a bit and began again.

"Ahem! Well, we're about to start the caroling section of

the festivities. I'd ask you to remember, we've had about ten minutes practice and we're relying on all of ye to join in and help cover up any mistakes. We're lucky to have a fantastic Soprano here, Margaret Fury and another local resident, Alvaro Aguilar who is actually studying music at the moment –" a rousing cheer from the crowd –"and is already quite a sought after Tenor. We also have Ciara Bailey -she's shy but wait til she gets singing! The rest of us will just try to keep up!"

An encouraging round of applause greeted this and Cullen continued. "So, first of all we're going to sing Once in Royal David's City, then The Wexford Carol and on to Curoo Curoo, or to give it its proper name, the Carol of the Birds. Um – yes, Margaret would like me to remind you all that you can google the words on your phones if you're unsure of them. No excuses for not singing out!"

The singing was tentative at first, and the old Wexford Carol was sung mainly by the older people, with the younger ones looking unsure. But when even the best singers, Alvaro and Margaret, laughed at their own mistakes, people began to forget their insecurities and the noise level rose accordingly.

Margaret tackled the Irish carol *Don Oíche Úd I mBeithil*, to a roar of approval as the last notes faded away and then to the delight of the children present, Jingle Bells started up. Ciara stepped forward, and everyone gasped at the huge, warm, bluesy voice that rang out across the night. Who could have guessed that tiny frame held such power? The impromptu choir had found its feet now, following up with modern songs and holiday favourites and soon members of the audience were shouting out suggestions. And as the laughter and good feeling swelled, Eve felt a sudden surge of joy and peace. She glanced over her shoulder, and in the dark, away from the glow of phones and torches, she saw three young people surrounding an antlered beast, its form too large and impossibly magnificent. As she watched it laid its head on Ashleigh's shoulder, and the two boys reached in to hug its neck.

"One more! One more!" the crowd shouted, to the protesting singers. "Gwon, one more!"

"Okay then," Cullen raised his hands. "Let's end on one for the kiddies and all among us young at heart….Santa Clause is Coming To Town!"

The kiddies, fresh from school concerts and plays, knew every word by heart and their parents, having suffered through several months of rehearsing for the same, were also confident. One little boy couldn't wait for the singers to begin, instead shouting out the opening lines with more aplomb than musicality, bringing a fresh wave of laughter and a disorganised but joyful start. Eve wanted to watch, with all her heart she wanted to stare and stare and see for sure, but some instinct – a pure, and simple impulse, a secret knowledge shared in childhood – made her turn resolutely away.

Whatever happened, she would choose to believe without seeing.

And as the last notes rose into the air, she felt a swoosh of wind, a breeze grazing her cheek, and to the delight of all the assembled, a burst of multicoloured sparkles illuminated the sky, followed by another and another and finally a glowing circle that hung in the night sky for a full minute.

After a moment of awed silence the crowd burst into loud applause and shrieks.

"Oh wow! I didn't know you had organized fireworks?" one

of the locals exclaimed.

Eve grinned. "You never know what will happen around here."

* * *

Mairead and Liam pulled up outside just as Eve reached Kimberly Cottage. The party was still going, with the last buns and cups of tea being passed around and lots of chatter. People were already talking about arranging another event, maybe to celebrate the new bank holiday in honour of Bridget, and she had left Tom chatting happily to a group of teenagers about sustainability and urban vegetable growing. But a text from her daughter saying she was only five minutes away had sent Eve hurrying home, her heart feeling very full.

"Mam!" Mairead hugged her tightly, and drew back, frowning. "Are you okay? Liam, get the bags out and bring mine upstairs. Leave yours in the living room – Mam, is he sleeping in the living room? Now, how have you been coping? What on earth has been going on here?"

Liam winked at his mother, behind Mairead's back. "She picked me up in town, Mam, and she's been giving out all the way here about this being Dublin's "murder hotspot." Fair warning, she wants you to sell up and move – immediately."

Eve patted the young woman gently on the back. "Stop it, Mairead. You don't know how much this place means to me, and it's not a murder hotspot. It's – just been a little unfortunate. That's all. Besides, there wasn't a murder here or even on Bramble Lane, this time. It was …in the local area, that's all."

Liam snorted, but backed her up.

"I told you, Mairead. There's nothing to worry about. Besides, Mam is well able to take care of herself. Oh wow! The tree looks amazing, I love it. Is that – is that the bauble I made in school? Where on earth did you find it. Look, Mairead – look! Yours is here too. I thought they'd been thrown out years ago…"

Mairead ran to see, and for a moment, as she touched the wee gaudy token, Eve saw the young girl with glasses, and a ponytail and gangling legs, proudly handing her the homemade decoration.

"You kept it."

"Of course I did. I would have put it out every year but – well, you know. Your dad. But from now on, they go on the tree. They're my favourites, you see." She held out her arms to them. "You're my favourites."

In a little while, Eve knew, her mother would descend on them eager to see her grandchildren. Her brother would arrive in, bearing presents and Tom would join them for tea. Dymphna, Claudia and Greta would make an excuse to pop in, and she'd probably have to turf them out in the wee hours of Christmas morning. She fully expected Ronan and Margaret to drop by – perhaps to show off a flashing, diamond ring on her left hand. She had last seen Cullen talking earnestly to Ashleigh's mother, and from the set of them, it wouldn't be a shock if they made their way to hers too, to prolong the evening. Ashleigh and Boyd and Sean – they were off out with Jenny Chan and her gang, Melly had been invited along too, so she'd be amazed if Finn and Ellen didn't end up at her kitchen table later.

But for now, right now, there was only her and her children and memories of Christmases long past…and the promise of better ones to come.

Folklore and Folk Magic

A huge theme in this book is the attitude toward the land, how it is seen as a living and sacred being, in Irish folk practices. As a largely agricultural society for most of our history, there is of course a special sense of connection to the land in Irish society. The many years of occupation and oppression, and the fight to be allowed to even own land, a right denied to us as indigenous Irish people, has intensified that connection.

In Irish mythology and ancient practices, there is a strong belief in the energy of the land. In modern Irish we refer to this as Brí - the natural energy of wild places - and Bua - the energy a place gets through human usage. The terminology may or may not be modern, depending on which scholar you like, but the concept is old. The ability to connect with both energies is a fundamental part of the role of the Wise Woman, the Bean Feasa (Ban Fahsa.) She would negotiate between the wild spirits, the Sidhe, (Shee) the otherworldly entities like Púca, (poohkah) and the human population. She would also be called on to correct or heal the Bua energy of buildings.

A Bean Feasa cannot fully translate into English but the nearest word is witch. She was a very important part of every Irish community, filling various roles. She was part healer, part advisor, feared and admired. She would negotiate between ordinary people and the otherworld entities like the Sidhe. She could charm and hex, and help break bad luck or curses.

She often stood up to the local Doctor, Landlord or Priest - and in the folklore, always bettered them!

Eve's ability to tune into both the land and the city, reflects both ancient and modern beliefs in community and the energy it produces. The ancient city of Dublin, my beloved home, is a very magical place in its own way. Its personality shines through even in the most modernized areas, and it is a guardian to those who live there.

Her ability to project her mind and "see" what's happening elsewhere, is in the tradition of the "Aisling" - predictive, or prophetic, dreams. This is also the name given to a branch of poetry, where the poet experiences a vision (usually of Ireland herself, in the form of an old woman, or a young maiden.)

Another useful skill displayed by the ladies is the ability to loosen tongues, and to use food as a tool to put people at their ease. Even ordinary people believed that you could put emotions into your cooking - a sour temperament would turn milk sour, a loving heart could pour love into the baking and so on. If you met with the fairies, the Good Neighbours, the Sidhe, you were warned to neither eat nor drink anything they offered.

The ability to sweet-talk and persuade comes under the Irish word "plámás" pronounced roughly *"plawe-__mawz__."* This can mean flattery but like many Irish words, defies direct translation into English. It really means an ability to butter up, soften up, convince, flatter, sweet-talk. The Irish "gift of the gab" in short!

If you run into Dymphna Moriarty, you're probably safe enough if you accept a slice of cake but if she starts asking you tough questions…you might be surprised how much you'll tell her!

In the early days of the Irish State, a project called the School's Folklore collection asked school children nationwide to collect folk tales and superstitions from their parents and grandparents. It is available online and is a fascinating insight into Irish culture. Among these funny, poignant records are countless examples of our shared belief in magic.

Http://www.duchas.ie

I hope you have enjoyed this short explanation of the Irish folk magic mentioned in The Kimberly Killing. All books in this series will come with extras like this, so please do follow me at my newsletter! https://mailchi.mp/c5d9815e1c52/newsletter-signup

I promise not to spam you and to provide some fun Irish news and insights as well as special offers and pre-order prices on books.

Also by Nina Hayes

The Kimberly Killing

First in the Old Bat Series.

Eve Caulton is looking forward to a new life in Kimberly Cottage - until a body turns up in her own living room.

Lucky for her, her mother Niamh, and the feisty senior ladies of Bramble Lane are on hand to offer help. And their unique skills - a magical, fun Irish cozy mystery filled with authentic Irish folk traditions.

The Music Shop Mysteries,

Writing as Geraldine Moorkens Byrne

Mrs O'Brien runs Ireland's oldest music shop and presides over her beloved West Stephen Street. When new landlords threaten her neighbours, she is prepared for the fight and when the hated estate agent is found murdered, she has to solve the mystery. Aided by her colleague, Michael and mad cap teen Mai, she recruits the Super Ukers Ukulele group and sets out to save the street!